WHICH WAY IS HOME?

WHICH WAY IS HOME?

Maria Kiely

Nancy Paulsen Books

NANCY PAULSEN BOOKS
An imprint of Penguin Random House LLC, New York

Copyright © 2020 by Maria Kiely

Nancy Paulsen Books is a trademark of Penguin Random House LLC.

Visit us online at penguinrandomhouse.com

Library of Congress Cataloging-in-Publication Data
Names: Kiely, Maria, author.
Title: Which way is home? / Maria Kiely.
Description: New York: Nancy Paulsen Books, [2020] | Summary: In 1948,
following World War II, eleven-year-old Anna, her mother, and older sister
must flee Czechoslovakia after Russian Communists take over the government.
Includes notes about the author's family history, on which the story is based.
Identifiers: LCCN 2019054096 | ISBN 9780525516804 (hardcover) |
ISBN 9780525516811 (ebk)
Subjects: CYAC: Family life—Czechoslovakia—Fiction. | Refugees—Czechoslovakia—
Fiction. | Communism—Fiction. | Czechoslovakia—History—1945–1992—Fiction.
Classification: LCC PZ7.1.K544 Whi 2020 | DDC [Fic]—dc23
LC record available at https://lccn.loc.gov/2019054096

Printed in the United States of America
ISBN 9780525516804

1 3 5 7 9 10 8 6 4 2

Map art and layout © 2020 by Ethan Crenson and Amanda Alic
Design by Suki Boynton • Text set in Sabon LT Std

For Nina & Sam

☙

Because as NaiNai says,
"This is the story of how you all came to be."

- CONTENTS -

SUMMER
1948

Chapter 1
STORMY WEATHER

I CAN FEEL the wind in my hair and hear rolls of thunder in the distance. I glance over at my cousin Maruska and see her large blue eyes shining with excitement.

"Look at those clouds! We're in for a big storm, Anna!" shouts Maruska. She's perched on the deck of our ship in her nightgown with bare feet, her long light-brown hair still tangled from sleep. I run over and try to grab her hand as Maruska, shrieking with delight, dives into the foamy sea.

"I'll save you!" I cry, leaping after her. We splash about in the frothy waves, taking turns jumping from the ship into the water. Suddenly Maruska's eyes widen with fear.

"It's my father! Look! He's fallen overboard! He's drowning! We have to do something!" she yells.

"Hold on! I'm coming!" I call.

The wind howls, and the waves grow higher and higher. I dive into the roiling sea, determined to save my uncle. My fingers graze his arm, which is just out of reach. I struggle to keep my head above the waves, and then, with one desperate lunge, I reach out and grab him. "I've got him!" Maruska is at my side, and together we pull him to safety.

We've just gotten him onto our ship when Maruska dives back into the water, this time calling out for my father.

"We'll save you, Papa!" I cry as I follow Maruska into the sea. It takes longer to find my father in the freezing water, but we will not let him drown. Maruska and I are the most powerful swimmers in the world. The sea is no match for us. Maruska grabs my hand, and together we dive under the waves, kicking our legs hard against the pull of the undertow.

Finally, just as the waves are about to claim him, I reach Papa and wrap my arms around his shoulders. Maruska helps me bring him to the ship, and soon we are safely on the deck. We lie flat, panting and trying to catch our breath, but then another wave as tall as a house crashes down upon us. We are all washed overboard, and Maruska and I will have to carry out another rescue mission. We are so brave. We can make it through any storm! Suddenly there is a crash of thunder so loud, it shakes the whole world. The storm stops.

Chapter 2
ROVEN

MARUSKA AND I freeze amid the pile of down comforters. My mother stands ashen-faced in the doorway.
Behind her are my aunt, my grandmother, and Franta
and Stepan, our two farmhands.

"Anna! Maruska! You're all right! What were you
doing?" my mother cries half in relief, half in anger.

We look up at them in surprise, and then I see the
clock on the wall. It's after nine. We've missed breakfast.
This weekend is the tenth anniversary of my grandfather's death, and lots of aunts, uncles, and cousins have
gathered at my grandparents' farm in Roven to celebrate
his life. My grandfather was an important man—not
just to us, but to our country—as he was prime minister
of Czechoslovakia before the war. I don't remember him
because he died when I was a baby, but I know he did
many great things for the country and was widely loved
and respected. There's going to be a Mass on Sunday
with lunch at the farm afterward, and everyone from the

village will come, but now I get to enjoy spending time with my cousins.

"I'm sorry, Mama. We were playing and lost track of time."

"Didn't you hear us knocking? We thought something terrible had happened. Franta and Stepan had to break down the door!" Mama exclaims.

"Babicka told me to bolt the door when she went over to the farm kitchen," I try to explain to Mama and Babicka and the farmhands. I had thought it a strange request, as I had always felt safe in Roven, even during the war, but now everything was changing with the Communist takeover. Not everyone in the village was a friend anymore.

"We thought the banging was just thunder. We're so sorry," whispers Maruska.

The grown-ups stare at us in confusion. The morning sun is shining brightly through the window.

"Aha. You were playing Storm at Sea again, weren't you?" Babicka says. "Didn't I tell you to get dressed and come have breakfast with us all right away?"

Maruska and I nod meekly. Babicka reaches up to smooth back a strand of loose hair. Her gray hair is usually tied back in a tight bun, but when she lets it down, I think how much she looks like Mama, with a soft round face and warm brown eyes that look kind even when she is upset.

"Well, no one can say you girls don't have good imaginations," Babicka says as she begins to laugh.

Soon everyone is laughing with her, including my mother, who wraps her arms around me. I notice my head reaches just below Mama's chin now.

"All right, then, get dressed. If you hurry, you can still have some buns before they're cleared away," Mama says, kissing me on the forehead.

Chapter 3
COUSINS

∽

AFTER BREAKFAST, MARUSKA and I run out to the
stables to find our cousin Pavel grooming the horses. He
is tall, with thick black hair and an easy smile. Pavel is
fourteen, three years older than me, but he never treats
me like a little kid, and he always defends me when my
older sister, Ruzena, tells me off. He starts laughing as
soon as he sees us.

"That must have been one crazy game of Storm at
Sea! I'm sorry I missed it. Hey, I've got a new joke.
Want to hear it?"

"Sure!" Maruska and I reply.

Pavel loves to make us laugh. During the war, he
collected anti-Nazi jokes and called them his own form
of protest. Even though that war's over, he still tells
them sometimes.

"A man walks into a records office and says, 'I'd
like to change my name.' The clerk says, 'Okay, what's
your name?' The man says, 'Adolf Stinkyfeet.' The clerk

says, 'I understand why you'd want to change it. What would you like your new name to be?' And the man says, 'Peter Stinkyfeet.' "

We all laugh and Pavel looks pleased.

"Are you almost done? We have so much to talk about." I stroke the nose of the chestnut mare Pavel was grooming.

"Yes, let's go!" Pavel hangs the horse brush on the wall hook with a flourish.

We grab our bicycles from the side of the barn and push off, leaving a cloud of dust behind us. I feel a burst of joy that it's summer and I'm finally with my cousins again. Pavel's family lives in Prague, while Maruska's family runs a hotel halfway between here and Prague. My family lives most of the time at Roven, and it's my favorite place to be—but when my cousins visit, it's even better.

I know this place well, and my mouth waters as we pass the farm kitchen and inhale the aroma of Babicka's delicious chicken soup. The comforting sound of Ruzena practicing a Chopin prelude floats through the open parlor window. Her first solo piano concert is in Prague next month, and she's determined that it will be perfect.

When we arrive at the village road, Pavel and I

pause to let Maruska catch up—sometimes I forget that she's only eight and her legs aren't as long as ours.

"I'm so happy it's summer vacation," I tell Pavel. "Did you have to listen to that minister of education guy on the radio at school? He got everyone really upset."

"Yeah, we had to listen to that propaganda. Every school was required to play it." Pavel imitates the minister's voice: "We are now building the Communist state, and you are the generation that will lead us. We will be victorious, but we have enemies who want to stop us. They are among your parents and your teachers. It is your duty to report them to the party."

"Stop. You sound just like him," I say. "We all thought his message was creepy—as if we'd ever become spies for the Communists!"

Pavel shakes his head, and when Maruska catches up to us, we're off again. When we reach the woods at the edge of the village, we park our bikes and head in deeper on foot. The leaves on the trees have filled in and the brook has widened into a stream, but when we reach our little fort, it's almost unchanged from when we were here earlier this spring.

This is our special spot. The place where Pavel and I—and now Maruska—come to get away. The place we share our secrets and our worries—but mostly worries lately.

We sit on rocks and I take a deep breath, inhaling the sweet and earthy scents of pine trees, moss, and mushrooms. A ragged handkerchief tied to a branch flaps gently in the breeze.

"Our flag's still here. I was afraid somebody might have torn it down," Maruska says, reaching up to touch the cloth.

"Nobody but us knows what it means," I remind her.

I think of the March day we came out here to hang it to honor the death of Jan Masaryk, the last man to stand for democracy in the new government after the Russian Communists took over. The Communist leaders claimed he'd killed himself, but we knew they had murdered him. Ruzena told me that Papa had proof. The Communist Party had pretended to support the Czech government at first—that's why they had let Masaryk keep his job—but really they didn't want anyone else to have power. Two weeks after Masaryk died, Papa took the evidence he had and left the country. Ruzena told me he's taking it to show the French government to ask them to help remove the Communists.

That was three months ago, and we haven't heard from Papa since. During the war, he also went into hiding, but he often snuck back to see us—now, with spies for the Russians everywhere, it's just too risky.

Pavel stands and removes his cap, holding it over his heart.

Maruska and I stand at attention next to Pavel, staring solemnly at the handkerchief. After a moment, we release our salute.

Pavel clears his throat. "Heavenly Father, we pray that you keep Anna's papa safe so that the truth may be revealed and the Communists will be . . ."

"Kicked out!" Maruska yells.

"And we can all be safe together again!" I say.

"Amen!" Pavel and Maruska both shout.

Chapter 4
SPIES EVERYWHERE

WE CAN USUALLY play for hours at our fort, but today our hearts aren't into any games and we decide to pick mushrooms instead.

Maruska wanders off in search of larger mushrooms, but I stay close to Pavel.

I lean toward him. "There's something I have to tell you."

Pavel stops and looks into my eyes. "What is it?" he asks.

"You know how when we stay in Prague, I like to bring Papa his lunch at the Department of Agriculture?" Pavel nods and I continue. "Well, one day in February, I'd just gotten off the train and was walking to his office when two men stopped me and started asking me questions about Papa."

"Had you ever seen them before?" asks Pavel.

"No, but I could tell they were Russian secret police,

so I acted like I didn't understand what they were talking about and walked away, but they followed me. When I got to Papa's building, I didn't want them to see which office I was going to, so I ran as fast as I could. I squeezed into the elevator just as it was closing and never saw them again."

"What did your papa say when you told him?"

"I didn't tell him. I was too scared. I didn't want to worry him. Now I'm afraid those men might have caught him."

"Don't worry—you did the right thing. Besides, I doubt those two could catch your father if they couldn't keep up with you! He's one of the smartest and bravest people I know," Pavel says. "Remember what a hero he was during the war?"

I smile with pride. Before the war, my father was a Czech diplomat in Paris. Then, when the Nazis took over and the Czech government had to go into exile in London, Papa acted as an Underground spy helping the British army fight the Nazis. Ruzena told me that the firefighters in our village let him set up a special radio to communicate with the BBC in the back of their fire truck. They'd drive him around late at night so he could find out where the Nazis had their weapons and report it to the British intelligence agents. Because of my brave papa, lots of weapons were destroyed and the Nazis were eventually defeated.

A twig snaps loudly behind us, and we look up with a start. Maruska is standing there grinning and holding a basket overflowing with mushrooms.

"Last one home is a rotten goose egg!" she cries, sprinting off toward her bike, and we follow her.

Chapter 5
SONGS OF HOME
⤲

BABICKA IS DELIGHTED by our crop of mushrooms. She makes them into a delicious sauce over chicken and knedlíky—her bread dumplings that are as soft and light as air. After dinner, the whole family gathers around the piano. Papa always used to play with Ruzena, but now only Ruzena sits down at the keys.

She begins to play "Koupím Já Si Koně Vraný," and we all sing along. Ruzena takes the harmony, and Mama and my aunts join in for the chorus. When we finish, everyone applauds.

"Your playing is wonderful. Your father would be so proud," Babicka says, laying her hand on Ruzena's shoulder.

Ruzena smiles sadly. "He always said he would be in the front row of every concert when I became a famous pianist."

I stare out the window wondering if Papa will ever

see Ruzena realize her dream, and then I hear a quiet sigh from beside me.

"Are you okay?" I whisper.

"I miss my father," Maruska whispers back.

I nod and squeeze her hand.

My father's only been gone for three months and it's been terrible, so I can't imagine what it's like for Maruska, who hasn't seen hers in years.

"Okay, what next?" Ruzena turns to us from the piano.

Pavel glances over at me and Maruska.

"'Nepudu Domů'!" he shouts. I know he is trying to cheer us up, and we all laugh as my sister begins the funny tune about the little boy who doesn't want to go home because he will be in trouble for eating all the noodles that his grandmother cooked for dinner. The whole family sings together, and Pavel dances about, doing his best impression of the naughty boy and the angry grandmother. We laugh until tears run down our cheeks.

"Okay, one more. What shall our last song of the evening be?" Ruzena asks.

" 'Zeleni Hajove,' for Papa," answers Mama. It is the song he always sings.

Mama and Ruzena sing together, and I try to join in, but my voice sticks in my throat.

I look around at all my relatives, thinking about how I am a part of so many generations of family members who have spent their lives connected to this place. It's where we always come back to. It's where we're from.

I won't sing this song till Papa comes home.

Chapter 6
WHOM TO TRUST?

ON SUNDAY MORNING, Teta J helps Maruska get dressed for church while I button up my best dress. I notice it's a little shorter than the last time I wore it. Mama will have to let down the hem again, but it'll do for today. I run my hairbrush through my straight brown hair and pull it back off my forehead with a red bow. I smile at myself in the mirror. Not as beautiful as Ruzena but cute enough.

Maruska and I hold hands as we run through the farmyard and down the main road, following our mothers to church. Two of the new lambs are very excited by us.

"Hi, lambies!" Maruska calls.

"Do you want to come to church with us?" I shout. The lambs jump about and bleat as if they are answering me. "Okay, then you have to walk like this." I skip, and the lambs seem to copy me. Maruska and I almost fall over, we are laughing so hard.

Ruzena gives us a disapproving look as we find our places in the family pew. Pavel catches my eye and does a remarkably good impression of Ruzena, and we dissolve into laughter again. Pavel leans over to whisper to us, and I am about to move toward him when I see Babicka's face. She looks so solemn that I know now is not the time.

⌒

After the service, people line up to greet my grandmother outside the church. Maruska and I stand together behind Babicka and watch as several men in formal Czech military uniforms take turns bowing low over Babicka's hand.

"Stop gaping at them!" Ruzena whispers harshly. "Don't you know who they are?"

I shake my head, and Ruzena gives an exasperated sigh. "They're members of the Czech government who resigned rather than work for the Communists. They're here to pay their respects to Babicka and Dedecek, and show that they stand for the old democratic Czechoslovak government. They're making a brave statement."

I nod. It feels like danger is closing in all around us and we are not even free to be ourselves. I watch my mother and aunts talking to the men. Their faces look very serious.

Maruska and I follow Ruzena down the path from the door of the church to the cemetery. We come here every week to tend the family graves—replacing the dead flowers with fresh ones and watering the plants. The cemetery is usually a peaceful place, and I enjoy keeping it beautiful, but today the mood is very solemn. As I look at all the flower arrangements surrounding my grandfather's grave, death feels very close and real. I miss Papa terribly. Nothing feels right without him.

I spot Pavel filling a watering can at a spigot in the wall and go to join him. "Everyone seems so tense now," I say.

"I know what you mean," Pavel replies. "I think it's hard to know whom to trust when the Communists want everyone to spy on each other and report anyone who isn't on their side."

I shuffle my feet, kicking a few pebbles down the drain in the ground.

"Pavel, remember when the war was finally over and the Nazis were gone and the Russian soldiers drove their trucks and tanks down the main street?" I ask.

Pavel nods.

"We were really happy to see them. We picked lilacs and threw them at them. I thought they were the good guys."

"Sure, I remember," he says. "We were grateful they helped beat the Nazis and end the war. We didn't know we'd be released from one brutal government only to be taken over by another."

"Yeah, we were so hopeful things would go back to normal," I say. "No more roundups of people who resisted . . ."

"No more . . ." Pavel sticks his finger under his nose like a mustache and goose-steps around me in a circle like Hitler. I know he's trying to distract me from my worries, but nothing seems funny now.

"It's gotten scary around here again now," I murmur. "Ruzena told me that anyone who doesn't side with the Communists will be sent to prison camps or even killed. Do you think that's true?"

Pavel sighs and nods again. "I think so. I've heard my parents saying things like that at night when they think I'm asleep."

"Of course it's true!" I jump at the sound of Ruzena's voice. I didn't realize she was standing nearby.

Ruzena is only two years older than Pavel, but she talks to us as though we're just little kids. She puts her watering can under the spout and lowers her voice so it's barely audible over the sound of the running water. "The Russians want to turn us against each other. They were very tricky, pretending they were on the side of democracy at first, but all they wanted was to use us. Why do you think Mr. Z's always prowling around the farm even though he was fired? He wants to gain favor with the Communists by reporting on our family. He knows we'll never be loyal to them."

"Ugh! I hate that guy! He sure went quickly from being Hitler's best friend to being a good little Russian comrade," Pavel says through gritted teeth. "It was the best day ever when Babicka fired him!"

"I hate him too," Ruzena replies. "But since he got fired from our farm, he has it out for us even more! He'd be rewarded if he could turn Papa in. You know how badly they wanted a war hero like our father to join their party—and how much they'd love to punish him as an example to anyone else who'd dare to resist them."

"But Mrs. Z was always nice to us. She wouldn't let Papa be sent to jail. Would she?" I say, trying to control my voice so that Ruzena won't hear the tears welling up in my throat.

"I don't think Mrs. Z would be able to stop him.

It's not like he ever cared about what she wanted anyway."

Ruzena turns off the tap, picks up her watering can, and marches off across the cemetery, leaving me in shocked silence.

Pavel wraps his arm around my shoulder. "Don't worry. Mr. Z and his comrades are no match for our family."

Chapter 7
BRAVE ANNA

AFTER LUNCH, MARUSKA, Pavel, and I play fetch with my dog, Gar. Gar's an excellent retriever, and no matter where we throw the stick, he always comes tearing back across the lawn with it in his jaws.

"Look how far I can throw this," Pavel boasts with a grin. He releases the stick, and it flies over the fence. "Okay, puppy, let's see if you can get that one."

Pavel must have thrown the stick really far into the field, because Gar doesn't return right away.

Then *bang*! The sound of a gunshot shakes me to my core.

We hear Gar's yelp of pain. Maruska turns and races toward the barn, but Pavel and I run to the gate. We are met by Gar, who leaps into my outstretched arms, trembling violently. Blood is soaking the tip of his ear. I stroke his silky brown fur, trying to calm him down.

A familiar voice chills my blood. "Keep your nasty dog off my property," Mr. Z walks over and snarls at me.

I want to scream for Mama, but feeling Gar shaking in my arms, suddenly brave Anna from the storm takes over. I step forward and say in a voice I hardly recognize, "How dare you hurt my dog!"

"That dirty animal was digging in my field. I could have killed him if I'd wanted to. Remember that, little girl," Mr. Z growls. He is still clutching his gun, and I can't take my eyes off it, but somehow I keep talking.

"He's not a dirty animal! And now you're on our property, so get out!"

Mr. Z laughs. "Your property, eh? We'll see how long that lasts." He spits on the ground and turns to go. Just as Mr. Z reaches the gate, he turns back and says, "By the way, how's your father, little girl? Tell him I'm looking for him." And then he's gone.

"Anna, you were amazing!" Pavel says to me. "You were so brave! See, I told you he was no match for you!"

"I can't believe I just did that!" I exclaim, looking up at him in shock. "What if he had shot me?"

My arms ache from holding my dog, so I carefully

set Gar down. I sink to the ground beside him just as Stepan appears at my side.

"Are you okay?" he asks. "Maruska told me what happened. Let me see the dog." Stepan begins to examine Gar gently.

"Is he going to be okay?" I ask, unable to keep my voice from shaking.

Stepan nods. "He'll be fine. It's just a small nick on his ear. I'll take him back to the barn to clean the wound." Stepan carefully lifts Gar.

"Good dog. Go with Stepan," I whisper, patting his back, and he stops trembling.

I want to go with them, but my legs feel too weak, and a new wave of terror hits me. I turn and grab Pavel's arm.

"What did Mr. Z mean, 'We'll see how long that lasts'?" I ask. "Do you think he's going to try to get the Communists to take away our farm?" I know this could happen because we've already seen them seize property from families we know.

Pavel takes my hand. "No chance. You really stood up to him. He won't be back anytime soon."

My shoulders start to relax, but I know Pavel's just trying to comfort me.

I lean forward and give him a hug. "I'm going to miss you so much when you go to Boy Scout camp!"

"I'll miss you, too, but I'll be back at the end of summer."

We sit together for a while, listening to the horses rustle in the stable. Pavel picks blades of grass and releases them into the breeze. As I watch them float away, I think about how cruel Mr. Z has become.

"Pavel," I say. "Do you think Mr. Z was the one who turned in Maruska's father to the Nazis during the war?" I ask.

Pavel looks sad at the mention of our uncle. "Maybe."

Then I ask something I have never said aloud. "Pavel, do you think our uncle is dead?"

Pavel takes a deep breath and slowly nods. "Unfortunately, I don't think the Nazis would have let anyone who tried to overthrow them live. And if he had escaped, he would have come home after the war. Alive or dead, he's a real hero, you know. All the Czech Resistance fighters are." Pavel brushes the back of his hand across his eyes, and I know he doesn't want me to see his tears.

I nod and bite my lip to hold back my own tears and ask the questions that scare me the most. "What about Papa? Do you think he's okay? Do you think I'll ever see him again?"

This time Pavel leans forward and looks intently into my eyes. "Anna, your father left at just the right time, and I'm sure he is being very careful. He has a lot of connections, and I'm sure he is safe wherever he is."

I want to believe what Pavel says so badly.

I want to believe that Papa is safe. That our country—and my family—*will* be okay.

Chapter 8
GEESE & STRAWBERRIES
～

"MAY I OFFER you more tea, Mrs.?" I ask, holding out the china teapot to Maruska.

"Yes, thank you, Mrs.," she replies as I fill her cup with water.

"And how is your dear little daughter today?" I ask.

"Oh, quite well. Thank you for asking. Her fever has gone down, and I think the medicine is working nicely," Maruska says as she lovingly strokes the hair of the doll sitting next to her.

"And how is your little girl, Mrs.?"

"Oh, she is very well too. Only, she will not sit up straight at tea," I say, adjusting my doll so that she leans against the back of her chair.

We are having one of our many dolly tea parties in the gazebo in the middle of the garden. Ruzena says I'm too old to play with dolls. That might be true, but I still have a lot of fun playing with Maruska—and she loves it, so I don't want to give it up.

A soft mist is falling, but the air is warm and fragrant, and we are enjoying being outside. I spread jam on a piece of bread, and Maruska helps herself to another cookie that Babicka baked for us. It is still such a treat for us to eat sugar, since it was so rare during the war.

Maruska looks out across the lawn. "Do you think it's dry enough to do some routines from the Slet?"

"Maybe I could do some of the dances, but it's probably too slippery to do any gymnastics. I could show you how I ate spinach again," I say.

Maruska bursts out laughing. "Yes! Show me!"

I put a cookie on my plate and look at it curiously. I pretend to cut it into tiny pieces with a fork and knife, and then I place a single crumb in my mouth. I wrinkle my nose, widen my eyes, then swallow, smile, and bow. Maruska applauds enthusiastically.

"Hooray!" she cries. "I think eating spinach for the first time might have been your favorite part of the Slet," she says with a laugh.

Maruska loves hearing stories about the week I spent in Prague at the Czech national gymnastics festival. Performing with my gymnastics troupe, or Sokol group, was one of the most exciting things that's ever happened to me. It was a very special event because this was the first Slet in ten years, since the Nazis didn't allow them to take place during their occupation. My Sokol group was invited to attend along with groups from all over Czechoslovakia. We got to wear uniforms with our name, group, and town embroidered on them. Ruzena performed with her Sokol group, too, and Maruska and I couldn't wait for her to be old enough to participate as well.

"Come say goodbye, girls!" Mama calls from the front steps of the house. I sigh. It seems like everybody is leaving. Mama is taking Ruzena to Prague so she can prepare for her concert with her piano teacher. Pavel's parents took him to camp a few days ago. Teta J has to go back to work at the hotel today, but at least Maruska gets to stay at Roven with me.

Maruska and I run across the lawn hand in hand. We haven't talked about it, but I know that neither of us wants to be alone in case Mr. Z comes back. It feels safer to stick together.

Mama is hugging Babicka goodbye, and I notice that neither one seems to want to let go. When they see me, they open their arms to include me in their embrace. I snuggle in between Babicka and Mama and breathe them in. Mama smells of the lavender perfume she always uses, and Babicka smells of flour and yeast from the bread she has been baking. I feel cozy and safe. I wish I could stay like this forever.

Once they've left, Maruska and I return to the gazebo for our dolls.

"Come on, Mrs., the rain has stopped. Let's take our girls for a walk," Maruska says as she settles her doll into the toy baby carriage we share.

"Yes, Mrs., let's take them to see if the strawberries are ripe yet."

"Splendid idea, Mrs."

I tuck my doll next to Maruska's, and we set off across the lawn, each pushing one handle of the carriage. Gar follows at my heels. Halfway across the lawn, I see a small flock of white geese pecking at the grass.

"*Husy, husy, husy,*" I call out. Maruska laughs because she knows what will happen next. As soon as they hear my voice, the geese lift their heads and look in our direction.

"Nice little geese," I call. "What good pets you are."

"They're not pets." Maruska giggles. "They're farm animals."

"You know they're my pets. Watch this. *Husy, husy, husy,*" I call again as we get nearer, and the geese line up single file and hurry over to follow me. I waddle at the head of the line, and the geese copy me. "What good little geese!"

"How come animals always do what you tell them?" Maruska asks as she runs next to us, pushing the doll carriage.

"Because they're smart," I joke as I lead my gaggle of geese across the grass.

As we near the strawberry patch, the air is perfumed with the sweet smell of ripe fruit. I breathe a contented sigh. I have to close the gate so that the geese will not get into the strawberries.

"Sorry, guys, you know you're not allowed in here, but here's a treat." I throw them a handful of cookie crumbs, and they snap them up. Maruska and I kneel in the damp grass, chatting and eating the small red berries until our mouths and fingers are stained and our bellies are full.

Chapter 9
PRAYERS

∽

"LET'S LEAVE THE windows open tonight, Mrs. That way we can smell the strawberries in our dreams," I say to Maruska as we tuck our dolls into bed. Almost a week has passed since the berries first ripened, and their perfume is even more delicious now.

"Mmmm, yes," she replies. "I will dream of pancakes with strawberry jam for breakfast."

"Anna," calls Babicka from the next room, "are you girls ready for bed?"

"Almost," I answer. "We're just putting the dolls to bed."

"Just a few more minutes, and then I'm coming in to say good night," she calls back.

Putting our dollies to bed is not a simple process. Both dollies must have their hair brushed and braided, their faces washed, and their nightgowns put on. Then they have to be tucked into bed, and we have to sing and say prayers with them until they fall asleep.

I add another blanket to my doll's bed and fluff the pillow under her head. Gar is curled up on his pillow between my bed and the doll's bed, and I lay a blanket over him too. His ear has healed, but still I am very gentle with him.

"Let's say prayers before Babicka comes in."

"Okay," replies Maruska. She makes the sign of the cross on herself and then on her doll.

I do the same and then I begin. "God bless Babicka and our mamas, our aunties, and our uncles. God bless Pavel and Ruzena. God bless Papa, and please keep him safe and let me see him again soon. God bless Maruska. And God bless Gar and all the animals."

Maruska cuddles her doll and adds, "God bless Anna, and God bless my father, and please bring him back to me." I hug Maruska close. She has said that prayer every night since her father's been gone.

"Amen," we finish together.

As we hurry to climb into bed before Babicka comes in, we are startled by headlights shining through our window and the sound of a car in the driveway. People rarely arrive by car and even less frequently at night, unannounced. Gar lets out a sharp bark, and we rush to the window to see what's going on, but even before we can look out, the door opens and Teta J enters our room, followed by Babicka. Maruska throws herself into her mother's arms, delighted by this unexpected visit. It's only been a week since Teta J left, and we didn't expect her back until the end of the month.

"Mama! You're back! I missed you!" Maruska exclaims.

"I missed you too!" Teta J sits down and pulls Maruska onto her lap.

"Are you staying?" asks my cousin, full of hope.

"Not this time, my dear. I've just come to surprise Anna. She's going to go on a trip to visit Pavel at camp, and we have to leave right away."

At this, I leap off the bed. "Really?! We get to visit Pavel?! I'll get ready right now."

"Me too!" Maruska announces, jumping off her mother's lap and hurrying to open the closet.

Her mother follows her and gently closes the closet door. "No, darling, not you too. I'm sorry, but I can only take Anna."

Maruska whirls around, tears streaming down her face. "Why can't I go? That's not fair! I want to see Pavel!"

My aunt tries to hold Maruska in her arms, but Maruska struggles away, throwing herself onto the bed and crying bitterly.

"I'm sorry, Maruska, but you are too young to make the trip. Anna can go because she's older."

"She's only eleven," sobs Maruska. "That's only three years older! I don't want to stay here alone! I want to see Pavel! I never get to do anything!"

"It's only for a few days. I would look after her. Why can't she come?" I plead.

At this point, Babicka takes over. "Not this time, Anna. She just can't this time. Now, let's get you ready."

While my aunt tries to console my weeping cousin, my grandmother helps me put on my Sokol uniform, which is my favorite outfit. I feel proud as I look in the mirror and see myself in the skirt, blouse, and jacket that represent my gymnastics team. I straighten the kerchief around my neck and smooth my hair behind my ears. I think I look very grown-up. A few minutes later, I am hugging a tearstained Maruska goodbye. Gar lays his head in her lap, and I am glad that she will have him to keep her company.

"Don't worry. I'll be back in a few days and I'll tell you everything!"

As I go to hug my grandmother, I see tears in her eyes too. I give her a big hug and kiss.

"Don't be sad, Babicka," I say. "I'll be home soon. I promise."

She hands me a cloth satchel full of food.

"This is for your trip." She sighs.

I wonder why she is giving me so much food for just a few hours' journey on the train, but I nod and thank her and put the strap over my shoulder.

She takes my face in her hands and kisses my forehead.

"*Hodná holčička*, good girl," she whispers. "And may the good Lord keep you safe on your travels."

Chapter 10
AN UNEXPECTED JOURNEY

I SIT WITH my nose an inch from the windowpane, watching my reflection mingle with the scenery rushing past. I pretend the cows and horses are my thoughts leaping out of my head and into the countryside.

Teta J had to return her car to her hotel, so we spent the night there and got on a train to Prague first thing this morning. The fields and forests slip away, and I strain to see the dark outline of Prague Castle rising majestically above the city. Teta J sits straight-backed and silent, absorbed in a book, oblivious to me and the world outside the window.

By the time Teta J and I get off the train in Prague, it's midmorning and the rain has started again. It doesn't feel much like summer, and I'm glad to have my warm uniform jacket and thick knee socks as we walk through the slick cobblestone streets to the apartment that my family keeps for when my father works in the city.

Just as we approach our street, Teta J takes my hand and guides me in a different direction. I wonder where we're going, but for some reason I get the feeling I shouldn't ask. Maybe it's the way she's holding my hand so tightly or the anxious look in her eye, but something makes me go with her in silence.

A few blocks later, we arrive at our destination, and I recognize it immediately. It is the apartment building where my father's best friend, Dr. V, lives. My heart pounds with excitement. Maybe my father is there! I hurry up the stairs behind my aunt and hold my breath as she knocks on the door.

The door swings open, and Mrs. V stands there smiling.

"Hello! Come in, come in," she says, ushering us into the small front hall. Even from where I am standing in the doorway, I can see that something's not right. The apartment is in chaos. Clothing, books, and paintings are scattered everywhere in the rooms beyond the hall, and boxes and suitcases are piled by the door. We follow Mrs. V into the living room, where my mother and Ruzena are sitting on the floor sorting papers and books into more boxes. I look around the apartment, but my father is not there.

My mother rises to greet us, and as she hugs me, she says, "Anna, I need you and Ruzena to run an errand for me. Ruzena knows what needs to be done. Be a good girl and go quickly with her." Ruzena is already buttoning her coat and heading toward the door. I hand Mama the satchel of food from Babicka and hurry after my sister.

When we get out into the street, Ruzena takes me roughly by the arm. "Come on!" she says, pulling me along beside her as she rushes forward.

"Ow, let go! Where are we going?" I say, struggling to free my arm. Ruzena only tightens her grip and turns sharply into a narrow alley between two tall buildings. It is dark and empty in the cold wet alley, and I'm scared.

"What do you think is going on here?" Ruzena asks in a furious whisper. "Do you really think we're going to visit Pavel at Boy Scout camp?"

I look at her blankly.

"Of course we're not! We're leaving. We're going to escape from Czechoslovakia and the Communists and go find Papa. And here you are wearing this stupid jacket with your name on the sleeve. Don't you realize that if the Russians catch us trying to leave, they'll throw us in jail to punish Papa?" With that, Ruzena rips the badge off my sleeve and stuffs it down the sewer drain.

I feel as if all the breath has left my body. Is this real or is she just trying to scare me? And Babicka let me wear my uniform, so it must be okay—lots of kids wear them—but Ruzena always thinks she knows better. I can't find any words to respond, so I just let Ruzena lead me out of the alley and into the busy street. I walk in a daze beside her to the train station and up to the ticket window, where she buys three tickets without even looking at me.

Back at the apartment, my mother is all alone, and she's changed into a stylish brown suit and high heels. Her long hair is pulled up in a twist, and she's wearing some makeup. She looks like she's ready for a day of shopping in Prague, and once again I hope that maybe Ruzena was just trying to scare me. But as I walk farther into the apartment, a cold feeling creeps over me.

We haven't been gone for longer than an hour, and yet the apartment's completely empty. It looks as though no one's ever lived there. Three small suitcases stand near the door.

We each pick up a bag and follow my mother out the door in silence.

Chapter 11
TRAINS, BOOKS, AND GLOVES

I HOLD TIGHT to my suitcase as we walk toward the train station. Ruzena keeps close to Mama on the other side.

"We can walk at a quick pace, girls, but be calm about it. We don't want to draw attention to ourselves by looking like we're in a rush," Mama says in a low voice. She talks casually and keeps her face relaxed as if we are going on holiday and she's just chatting about the weather. "We'll be taking three trains, so pay attention and stay close to me. Everything will be all right. Just go along with everything I say and do, and please don't ask any questions."

Ruzena and I nod in silence. I try to return Mama's smile but can't quite manage it. I pick up a small, smooth pebble from the sidewalk and drop it into my pocket. If we really are leaving, I'm taking a piece of home with me.

We squeeze down the corridor of the train. It's so crowded I can hardly breathe. There's only one open seat in a six-passenger compartment, and Ruzena and I take turns sitting in it or on our suitcases, trying to take up as little space as possible. It's so stuffy that we keep the door of the compartment open to get a little more air. Mama stands in the corridor, just outside our compartment door, reading a book called *Wuthering Heights*.

Mama is usually quiet with strangers, but now she is talking to a man we don't know about the book she's reading and how she recently bought three pairs of kid gloves. He seems very interested in the gloves. I guess it's because it's so hard to find anything fancy like that these days. Maybe Mama's just trying to pass the time, but it is still very odd. When the man moves on down the corridor, Mama tells us we'll be getting off at the next stop.

The second train is just as crowded as the first, and again Mama has odd conversations with strangers. It's past dinnertime when we get on the third train. I'm sleepy and hungry, but Mama is talking to another man, and even though she is talking softly, I can hear her mention kid gloves again.

There aren't any available seats on this train, so I perch precariously on my suitcase surrounded by people who smell of sweat, rain, and tobacco. It's dark and raining outside, and I doze off until Ruzena shakes me awake to get off the train. Mama leads us to a car, and when we get in, she talks softly to the driver.

We've been traveling all day on a trip I didn't even know we'd be taking.

And now I don't know where we are or where we're going.

As the car pulls away from the train station, I squeeze the pebble I picked up in Prague until it makes a deep indent in my palm. It hurts, but I don't let go.

I'm trying so hard to hold on to home.

Chapter 12
HOTEL BLUE STAR

∽

THE CAR PULLS up in front of an old gray stone building. A peeling sign above the door reads HOTEL BLUE STAR. Ruzena and I are almost too exhausted to stand when we get out of the car, but Mama marches up the front steps of the hotel with a straight back and we follow.

A man behind a counter greets us and leads us up a narrow flight of stairs and down a dim hallway that smells like old cabbage soup. Even though the smell is unappetizing, I can hear my stomach growl. He unlocks the door to our room and gives my mother the key. There are two wide beds with down comforters on them, and I long to lie down. A small lamp on a low table between the beds gives the only light the room has to offer and sheds a warm glow. The man and my mother exchange a few words, and then he nods to us and leaves, closing the door behind him. Once we are alone, Ruzena and I collapse on the nearest bed.

"You girls must be starving," Mama says. "The hotel clerk says there is a restaurant downstairs. Let's go and have a proper dinner."

Ruzena and I revive ourselves at the prospect of a meal, and once we have washed our hands and faces, we follow Mama back downstairs. I wonder if the cabbage-soup smell reflects what will be served in the restaurant, but then Mama opens a door, and we enter a cozy dining room that smells of freshly baked bread. As we settle into our seats, I feel myself relax for the first time all day. Each of us orders the same thing: *vepřoknedlo zelo*—roast pork with dumplings and braised cabbage. The meal is as good as any my grandmother would make back home.

I can almost hear Papa complimenting Babicka. *"Thank you for another delicious meal," he says as he lays his napkin by the side of his plate. "The knedlíky was especially light and tasty."*

"You must thank Anna for that," Babicka replies. "She practically made the dumplings by herself."

Papa wraps his arm around me as I come to take his plate. "Well, thank you, madam! Only ten years old and already an accomplished chef. I'm impressed!" I snuggle with him for a moment, and he tells me, "Run those dishes to the kitchen, and then we'll take our walk."

Mama and Papa walk slowly, holding hands, and I skip ahead to the strawberry patch to see if there's any ripe fruit. As I run back with a handful of berries, I watch my parents—my tall, handsome father with his thick black hair combed neatly off his forehead and my graceful mother beside him. They have stopped in front of a large peony bush that is bursting with pink blossoms.

Papa loves to talk about nature, so I assume he is telling Mama something about the flowers, but when I draw nearer, I see how serious their expressions are. "But when do you have to leave?" I hear Mama ask.

"I'm not sure," Papa replies. Then he catches sight of me and smiles. "Mmmm, I hope you'll share some of those berries with me!" He and Mama each pop a berry into their mouths.

"Delicious! Thank you, Anna," Mama says. Papa takes my hand, swinging it back and forth as we continue our walk.

I am shaken from my memories when the waiter places a bowl of ripe strawberries on the table to end the meal. Just tasting one, I can hardly hold back my tears.

Back upstairs, we quickly pull on our nightgowns and fall into bed. One bed is meant for me and Ruzena and the other for Mama, but tonight I want to feel safe, so I get out of my bed, where Ruzena is already fast asleep, and stand at the edge of Mama's. She lifts the covers to let me in and wraps her arms around me. She kisses my hair, sings a quiet lullaby, and falls asleep.

I sink into the pillows, but I can't sleep because my mind keeps drifting back to Roven. What's Maruska doing now? Is she putting her doll to bed? Is she kissing Babicka good night?

Are they missing me the way I'm missing them?

Chapter 13
LEARNING HOW TO TALK

∽

THE NEXT MORNING, I'm awakened by a knock on the door. I sit up, rubbing my eyes.

Mama and Ruzena are already out of bed and dressed. Mama is reading her book, and Ruzena is staring out the window at the overcast sky. Mama carefully puts down her book and opens the door.

The man from the night before is standing in the doorway holding a tray with a plate of buns, three cups, and a small pot of coffee. Mama holds the door wide so he can enter. He places the tray on the low table and looks at me. I smile at him. I'm hungry for breakfast, and I'm glad there will be something warm to drink even though I'm not used to coffee without lots of milk.

"That looks good. Thank you," I say.

He smiles back. "You're welcome," he says, seemingly surprised I am talking to him. He turns to my mother. "It looks like today will be a good day for you to leave after all," he says softly. "It is pretty dark and the weather is bad. You should be able to travel unnoticed. The car will be outside in half an hour."

My mother nods and thanks him, and he leaves with a quick nod to us.

After we eat our breakfast, I put my Sokol uniform back on. I pack my nightgown into the bag that now holds everything I own. Besides my nightgown, there are only a few sets of underclothing, some knee socks, a pair of thick stockings, a blouse, a skirt, a warm sweater, and my best dress. There is also a small zippered case with my hairbrush, toothbrush, two hair bows, and two handkerchiefs.

Mama stands with her back to the door. "Now, before we leave, I must teach you girls a new way of speaking. You must learn to talk softly without actually whispering. If you whisper, it will draw attention, but if you simply talk softly, no one will notice or overhear what you say."

With that, Mama changes the register and volume of her voice. "From now on," she continues, "whenever we're in a place where someone might be listening, you must only speak like this." Her voice is soft but clear, and there is no breathy sound that comes with whispering. Ruzena and I try to imitate the way Mama speaks, and when she's satisfied that we've done it correctly, she says, "Good, you've got it."

"How can you tell if someone is trying to listen?" I ask.

"You can't, dear, and that's why we must be very careful."

Chapter 14
NO-MAN'S-LAND

I CAN FEEL the wind in my hair and hear rolls of thunder in the distance as we leave Hotel Blue Star. Even though I ate breakfast, I feel empty inside as I follow Ruzena into the back of a big black car. The seats are low, so I can hardly see up to the front, but I can tell there's someone wearing a hat sitting next to the driver. I wonder who he is, but just as I'm about to ask, the driver begins to talk.

"We will be driving through no-man's-land," the driver tells us.

I lean over to Ruzena. "What's 'no-man's-land'?"

"Shhh," she says, jabbing me with her elbow.

But the driver must've heard me, because he explains, "It's the area around the German border where no one's allowed to go nowadays. But there are a few villages near it where some elderly folks who were allowed to stay in their homes during the war still live. So as we pass through each village, if we are stopped by the police, you must say we are on the way to visit your aunt or uncle who lives there."

He begins to list the names of the villages and the people in each who are supposed to be our relatives if we get stopped—and my heart pounds. How will I ever remember all the things he's telling us?

When the driver has finished speaking, I turn to Mama. "What if I say the wrong name to the police and we get caught?" I ask.

"You just keep calm and quiet and everything will be all right. We'll be safe in Germany soon," Mama replies.

It seems strange to think that Germany's a place where we'll be safe now. During the war, it seemed like the scariest place imaginable, but now that Hitler's dead and the war's over, I guess I shouldn't think that anymore. Thinking of Hitler reminds me of Pavel's jokes, and I smile to myself as I look out the window. The lush green fields and distant hills remind me of the countryside around Roven, and I wish so hard that I was there on my bicycle with my cousins instead of in this car.

Then a terrifying thought occurs to me, and I lean toward Mama and ask, "What if Mr. Z comes to Roven looking for us and finds out we're gone? What will happen to Babicka? Will she be safe without us?"

"Your grandmother will be fine," Mama says. "She's been running that farm for a long time. She has Franta and Stepan and many others in the village to help her. Don't worry."

"I just wish she could've come with us—actually, I wish we could have stayed," I whisper. Mama pulls me close and pats my hair but doesn't say more.

We drive for another hour or so in silence. I watch Ruzena and wonder what she's thinking. I'd like to ask her if she's as scared and worried as I am, but I know she wouldn't tell me. I know she must be sad to miss performing in Prague. She had just gotten the most beautiful silk dress to wear to her concert. My grandmother's friend is an artist, and she hand-painted a pattern of apple blossoms onto the skirt. When Ruzena tried it on, everyone marveled at how gorgeous and grown-up she looked.

People always talk about how beautiful my sister is. They compliment me, too, but I know it's different. Ruzena and I are both tall for our ages, but that's where the resemblance stops. She has long, beautiful black hair that she wears pulled up in the most fashionable styles. My hair is light brown and cut in a bob to my chin. Her eyes are dark brown just like Mama's, and mine are light blue like our father's. Her cheekbones are high and her features are perfect. My cheeks are round and my skin is rosy. She always has a serious expression, and I'm usually smiling. Maybe when I'm more grown-up, I'll look more sophisticated and serious too. But probably not.

Suddenly I feel embarrassed. It seems silly to think about dresses and hair and concerts. But when I think about what's happening now, my eyes start to water. I roll my pebble between my fingers and focus on slowing my breathing like Babicka taught me in order to calm myself. Maybe thinking about small, silly things isn't so bad when your world's full of big troubles.

The car slows and comes to a stop by the side of the road. I peek out the window, afraid we've been stopped by the police. But there's no one there, just a thick forest on either side of the road.

The driver gets out and comes around to open the door for my mother, and we follow her out of the car. The person in the hat climbs out of the passenger side, and for a minute my heart pounds with joy because I would recognize that Boy Scout uniform anywhere.

"Pav—" I start to say, but the name dies in my throat when he turns to face us and my hope is crushed.

Chapter 15
HONZA

⌒

THE BOY IS taller and looks older than Pavel, closer to eighteen than fourteen. He's wearing the standard Boy Scout uniform, but his badges show that he's reached the highest level of Scouts. He has bright-blue eyes and wavy dark-blond hair. Even I can see how good-looking he is—and I hardly ever pay attention to boys. I know Ruzena thinks so, too, because I see her stand up straighter.

A man approaches from behind a tree. When Mama shows him her book, he gives a small nod. The driver tells us to hide among the trees, so we follow Mama with the Boy Scout to a thick patch of bushes. We crouch together in silence while the driver and the new man talk near the car. They seem to be arguing, and I'm worried something is wrong. They raise their voices for a minute, and we can hear the new man say, "I'm not the kind of person who leads innocent people into a trap!"

Trap? What does that mean? Was our driver only pretending to help us and now he's trying to make this new man turn us in to the Communists? I feel Mama's body tense next to mine and I wonder what she's going to do.

What can we do? Run away? Where would we go?

We're in an unfamiliar forest with total strangers. I look over at the Boy Scout. Why is he with us? Is he running just like us, or is he here to trap us and turn us in?

My heart is pounding so hard, I am sure everyone can hear it.

Then the driver gets back in the car and pulls away. We have no choice now. We have to go on.

The new man motions for us to come out of hiding and says in a hushed voice, "I'm your guide. You'll be traveling with me to the German border. It's only about three or four miles from here, but the terrain can be difficult." He eyes my mother's shoes. "So it may take us a few hours to get there. You must follow me as quietly as possible, and when I do this"—he moves his right hand in a slight waving motion down by his leg— "you must hide behind the trees as well as you can."

We all nod in understanding.

Then the Boy Scout leans in and whispers to Mama,

"My name is Honza. May I help you and your daughters with your bags?"

Mama smiles and replies, "That's very kind of you, Honza. This is Anna and this is Ruzena. We're able to carry our own bags at the moment, but we'll be grateful for your help if the walking becomes more difficult."

We walk single file through the forest, where there's barely a path and it's hard to know where to step. The guide tries to avoid the really thick foliage, but there are lots of brambles and what seems like an obstacle course of roots and rocks. I watch Mama as I try to keep my balance and am impressed. I had almost forgotten what an excellent gymnast she was when she was younger. Despite her high heels, she's able to keep up with the guide—as if she's used to hiking in her best shoes.

I try to pretend we're just out on a regular hike. Not on a journey with a boy we don't know, following a man we have no reason to trust.

I look up and Honza smiles at me. Suddenly he doesn't feel like a stranger anymore, and I decide it's a good thing he's with us.

Chapter 16
HIDING

WE'VE BEEN WALKING for about twenty minutes when we hear a crackling sound up ahead. Our guide gestures for us to hide, so we crouch behind a clump of pine trees.

As panic rises inside me, I reach for Mama's hand and try to focus on the sounds of two birds calling back and forth in the branches above. I'm tempted to peek out from behind the trees when our guide reappears and motions to us to keep going.

As we walk, our guide occasionally gestures for us to take cover, but time after time, there is nothing and we continue on our way. I'm not as frightened now when we have to hide.

I'm lagging behind and wondering how much farther to the German border and what it will look like when I realize that Mama, Ruzena, and Honza are hiding behind a large bush just ahead.

I duck behind the nearest tree and feel my heart

freeze. There, standing with his back against another tree trunk, just a few feet away from me, is a police officer—a police officer who looks terrifyingly familiar.

Could he be one of the officers who chased me to Papa's offices in the streets of Prague?

He looks straight at me, and I think I'm going to faint. So many ideas flash through my head. Should I call out to my mother? Scream for the guide?

No, none of that will help me with this officer.

I know I have to be brave. And that I can*not* let him take us back.

So I look *him* right in the eye. I pray with all my heart, "Please, God, don't let him take us back. Please let us go on. Please keep us safe."

He returns my gaze for a long time and then, just as the guide comes out and waves for us to keep going, the policeman nods at me, and I know he's letting us go. We walk on and he doesn't say a word.

I look back again and I realize I've never seen him before in my life—and I feel like I've just experienced a miracle.

I wonder what would have happened if he had stopped us. Would we have been arrested? Sent to a work camp in Siberia? I can't even imagine what that would be like—and everyone says I have a good imagination.

Chapter 17
THE BORDER
⌒

IT FEELS LIKE we've been walking for ages when we reach the top of a hill and the guide announces that we're almost at the border. Now there's a less overgrown path to follow. Going downhill is a little easier, but the ground is wet and slippery in places, so it's hard to keep our footing. Ruzena loses her balance and begins to fall, but Honza catches her. He holds her hand for a moment longer than necessary, and even in the shadows of the trees, I can see my sister blush.

My knee socks are soaking wet, and my feet are cold and sore, so I try to keep my spirits up by imagining a warm bath with sweet-smelling bubbles.

Then, a few yards ahead of us, I see a large stone monument. It seems strange and out of place in the woods.

"Mama, what's that?" I ask in my low voice, pointing at the stone column engraved with a list of French names and a date from 1812.

"It's a monument in honor of the Napoleonic soldiers who died along this path trying to get home to France from where they were fighting in Russia in 1812."

A shiver passes through me as I think of the soldiers dying along this path. All they wanted was to go home. Just like me.

Ruzena moves closer to me, and we stand side by side looking up at the monument. Mama makes the sign of the cross, and Ruzena, Honza, and I do the same. Our guide watches us and quickly crosses himself too.

The clouds part and the sun streams through the trees, making the forest shimmer. It feels like a holy place. I wonder how many people have stopped here on their search for safety. I say a silent prayer for all of them and for us—that we *will* find it.

We walk on and follow the path a little bit farther. Then our guide stops and turns to Mama. "I'm sorry, madam, but this is where I must leave you," he says.

Mama stares at him in surprise but replies in a calm voice, "But you promised to take us to the German border."

"This is the German border," he responds, and I can't help looking around for the line on the ground that separates Czechoslovakia from Germany.

"I was told you would take us to the German post," Mama says firmly.

"I'm sorry. I cannot go on. You are in Germany now and the post is close by. Please understand it isn't safe for me to go farther. I can't risk being caught coming back across the border. I have a wife and family," he says as he looks pleadingly at Mama, and after a moment, she nods.

Our guide looks relieved. "Now, all you must do is follow this path for another mile or so, and you will come to the German post. You should be there in less than an hour."

Honza places his rucksack on the ground and begins to search around inside it. "Excuse me, sir," he asks, "but exactly which direction are we supposed to walk in?"

"Southwest," the guide replies, and Honza nods in thanks.

Mama reaches into her bag and takes out her wallet and *Wuthering Heights*. She tucks all of her Czech money into the pages of the book and hands it to the guide.

"Take this. It will help you get home safely. Thank you for your service," she says. He takes the book, bows his head, and then he is gone.

As I watch this exchange, a sudden wave of understanding washes over me. Mama must be using codes to help us escape. It dawns on me that every time she talked to strangers on the train about buying kid gloves, we changed trains. It was like the men were telling her where to go. And *Wuthering Heights* must be part of the code, too, because she was always reading it and showing it to people we met, and then she gave it to our guide and said it would help him get home safely. It's just like in a spy novel—kind of exciting but also scary.

As soon as our guide is gone, the forest seems much bigger, and I clench my fist tightly around my pebble.

Honza is looking for something in his rucksack. "I can't find my compass," he tells us. "But that way is north."

"How can you tell?" I ask.

Honza points to a patch of moss growing on one side of a large rock. "The sun is a good guide and so is the moss—it usually grows on the shadier, northern side."

"Impressive. You can be our compass from now on," Ruzena says.

Chapter 18
THE RAVINE

WE WALK SINGLE file, but this time Mama leads the way and I walk right behind her with Ruzena and Honza following. We don't get far before we hear the loud sound of rushing water. Mama stops abruptly, and I immediately see why. There before us, cutting its way through the forest—and across our path—is a deep ravine. Water is gushing through it and there is no way around it.

Mama wrinkles her brow and looks around. "This can't be right. We have been walking on the path just as he said we should, and he didn't mention crossing a ravine."

"Maybe it's a trap. Didn't our driver say something about that? Maybe the police are waiting in the trees to capture us. Maybe . . ." My sister is beginning to panic.

"No, Ruzena, we must not get hysterical worrying about traps. Perhaps he didn't mention it because there isn't usually so much water here. After all, it's been a very rainy summer. There is nothing to do but figure out a way forward," Mama says. She's so calm and brave, I believe we will find a way to go on.

"I can go back a bit and see if there is another way," offers Honza.

Then I see it and I know what we're supposed to do. "Look, Mama." I point to a log lying across the ravine a few meters downstream. "We can go across."

The log looks sturdy and like it was placed there on purpose. As we approach it, Ruzena starts shaking her head. "Oh no. No. I can't possibly walk across that. It's way too narrow. We'll fall. We'll be killed. I'm not even supposed to be here! I should be playing piano in a concert in Prague!"

Her voice starts as a whisper, but by the end, she is almost shouting and tears are forming in her eyes. Mama steps toward her and opens her mouth to speak, but Honza takes Ruzena's hand.

"No, no, this will be fine. I promise. I'll help you cross, no problem. We do challenges like this in Boy Scouts all the time. I can tell from Anna's uniform that she's good at gymnastics, and I bet you are too. It will be just like walking the balance beam. It will even be fun! Look!"

He scoops up Ruzena's suitcase and strides out onto

the log. Within seconds, he reaches the other side. "See, easy," he says, and returns for Mama's and my bags.

Once he has delivered our luggage to the other side of the ravine, he returns to help each of us across one at a time. First, he offers Mama his hand, and she follows him very slowly but with perfect balance across the log.

Next, it is my turn. Before I step onto the log, I foolishly look down into the swirling water and can't go on. I want to be brave, I really do, but it's too high and the water looks dangerous.

"Can't I just crawl across?" I whisper to Honza.

Honza crouches down, looks into my face, and speaks in a low, reassuring voice. "You don't want to crawl, Anna. That will be more difficult. You can walk across. I know you can. I won't let you fall. I promise. Just don't look down. Look straight at me. It will be fine. Trust me."

With that, he gives me a smile, takes my hand, and walks out onto the log in front of me. His hand is warm and strong, and I know I will be okay. A minute later, I am standing next to Mama, who takes me in her arms and hugs me with relief.

Honza goes back for Ruzena, who is watching nervously with her back against a tree trunk a good distance away from the edge of the ravine. When he reaches her, he bows with an over-the-top flourish and extends his arm to her with his head still lowered. I see her smile, and if the water had not been so loud, I might have even been able to hear her giggle. Honza leads Ruzena to the log as if they are walking to the middle of a dance floor. When they reach the edge of the log, Honza releases her arm. I see him say something as he takes my sister's hand and bows deeply over it. When he straightens, they are both smiling and she's blushing again. He leads her across and she follows him with complete confidence, as if she had never been afraid.

I'm amazed by how easily Honza helped each of us push our fears aside—maybe we're braver than we think.

Chapter 19
MUD

"I CAN'T BELIEVE we made it!" I exclaim as we catch our breath on the other side of the ravine. "Maruska and I pretend to do brave things like this when we play Storm at Sea—but I never thought I'd really have to do anything like this!"

"What's 'Storm at Sea'? Honza asks.

"It's a game my cousin and I play where we have to save people from drowning in a terrible storm that's wrecking our ship."

"Well, you are pretty good at being brave in real life," Honza says.

I'm surprised when Ruzena smiles at *me*, and I feel the warmth of pride fill me up.

"Now," Honza says, turning to Ruzena, "tell me about the concert you're supposed to be playing at."

"I'm a pianist and I was going to have my first solo concert in Prague, but then we had to leave . . ." Ruzena trails off.

"I'm sorry you had to miss it," Honza says. "I'd love to hear you play someday."

"I'd like that too," Ruzena tells him. "Do you play an instrument?"

"No, I took recorder lessons for a few months when I was eight, but then I lost my recorder and I haven't played since."

"Oh, that's too bad."

"Actually, I think my mom threw it away. I was terrible."

Ruzena laughs with Honza, and I marvel at how happy she seems around him.

Now that everyone has settled down, Mama starts walking and we follow. The path on this side of the ravine is wet and muddy. Mama takes a few steps, trying to avoid the worst spots, but she suddenly lurches forward and almost falls. Honza reaches out to steady her, and when she pulls her foot up, her shoe is missing. It has sunk so deep into the mud that none of us can see it.

Honza helps Mama to a dry place, and she stands against a tree while Honza, Ruzena, and I crouch around the puddle searching for her shoe and trying not to get stuck. The mud is thick like clay, and it makes loud sucking noises as we scoop it aside. Finally, my fingers grasp the heel of my mother's shoe and I proudly pull it from the muck.

It is almost unrecognizable, but Honza wipes it with some large leaves and Mama is able to put it on again.

"You're a mess!" Ruzena exclaims. But she says it in a gentle, teasing way that makes me smile, not in her usual know-it-all big-sister way.

"A little dirt never hurt anyone," I say.

"Well, then," Honza says, handing me a pile of fresh leaves. "May I offer you a washcloth from our finest collection, mademoiselle?"

He and Ruzena try to help but only succeed in spreading more mud all over me—and some on themselves. We collapse into fits of laughter, and I almost feel like I'm playing with Maruska and Pavel again.

Finally, Mama comes to the rescue when she finds two handkerchiefs in her bag. She dips them into a fairly clean puddle of water. "Wipe off as much mud as you can with the leaves, and then you can use these for your hands and faces."

"I have some water in my canteen," Honza offers.

"Thank you, Honza," Mama says. "But let's save that for drinking. The puddle water is fine to wash with."

While Mama helps me clean off, I watch Honza and Ruzena. Honza says something that makes my sister smile as he wipes her cheek with the handkerchief, and she takes it back and tries to rub some mud off his nose.

"Okay, I think we're all as clean as we're going to get for now," Mama says, looking us over. "We should start walking."

She turns back toward the muddy path, but I notice a narrow road through the trees. "Why don't we take that road? It seems to go parallel to this path and doesn't look as muddy. We should be safe—we're in Germany now."

"I like the idea of no mud," Ruzena says. "But are we sure it will lead us to the German post?"

"Both roads seem to go in the same direction," Honza says. "I think we should try it and keep our eye on the path too." He slings his satchel over his shoulder and picks up Ruzena's bag. "May I take your bag too?" he asks my mother.

"No, thank you. I can manage. Just help the girls if they need it," she replies.

"Your loyal pack mule at your service," Honza says to me with a grin. He reaches out for my bag, but I hold the handle tight. For some reason, even though my arms are tired, it makes me feel safer to carry my own bag.

"No, thanks. It's okay—I can carry it myself."

I don't want to hurt his feelings, but I can tell by the look in his eyes that Honza understands why I don't want to give him my bag.

"Anna, brave—and strong!" he says.

Chapter 20
ROAD TO NOWHERE

THE ROAD'S ONLY a little wider than the path, but it's much easier to walk on. As we walk, we can see a few other trails weaving in and out of the trees, but we seem to be heading in the same direction as our original path, so we keep going.

We travel for about an hour, but no German post comes into sight.

"Mama, didn't the guide say it was only a mile to the post?" Ruzena inquires. "We've gone much farther than that by now."

"Maybe he was mistaken and it's really more like two miles, but I'm sure we'll be there soon."

My throat is parched and my legs ache. I wish we could sit and rest. Streaks of sunlight reach between the trees and play on the road. It's beautiful, and I try to let it distract me from my discomfort. Honza is walking a little ahead of me, and I hurry to catch up with him.

"Do you have all the Boy Scout badges? My cousin Pavel is a Boy Scout, too, but he still has a lot of badges left to get."

"I have almost all of them. I was working toward the last one in boating just before I left, but I didn't have the chance to get it."

"What do you have to do to get the boating badge?" Ruzena asks.

"My friends and I were building a canoe, and we were supposed to take it down the Vltava." A look of sadness passes over Honza's face when he mentions his friends.

"What's the matter?" I ask.

"I'm worried about my friends. We were supposed to leave together, but I got delayed. They went without me, but I don't know what happened to them."

"Why'd *you* have to leave?"

"What delayed you?"

Ruzena and I speak at the same time, so the words come out in a jumble.

"I was originally going to leave Czechoslovakia with my family," Honza tells us. "My grandfather worked for the government, but he resigned when he realized the Communists weren't going to allow a real democracy to be reinstalled. He decided it'd be best for all of us to go before things got worse. But then my father got jailed for speaking out against a Communist official, and it was arranged for me to leave with my Boy Scout leader and some of my friends who'd gotten into trouble for protesting. On my way to the train station to meet them, I got stopped by Russian police. They asked me lots of questions about my family's political views, but I pretended I didn't know anything. I guess I played dumb so well, they finally gave up on me and let me go. But by that time, I'd missed the train and my friends were gone."

"Oh my goodness! The same thing happened . . ." I catch myself, worried that Ruzena or Mama will ask me what I'm talking about, but fortunately, at that moment, Ruzena cries out.

"Look," she says, pointing through the trees to where an elderly woman is picking mushrooms. "Shall I go ask her where we are? Maybe I can find out how much farther it is to the German post . . . if we're even going in the right direction—"

But my mother cuts her off. "No, Ruzena. You mustn't speak to her. We can't let anyone see us." Mama ushers us behind a cluster of bushes by the side of the road.

"But why?" I ask softly. "What harm could come of

asking a woman for directions? Isn't it supposed to be safe for us in Germany now?"

"First, we don't know exactly where we are," Mama says. "We haven't come to any official post yet. Second, even if we are in Germany, during the war, the Nazis convinced most Germans that Czechs were enemies and that they should hate us. That woman could very well still believe that and send us in the wrong direction."

As Mama speaks, I feel my stomach tighten. Another person who might send us into a trap.

It's getting harder and harder to believe that we could ever trust anybody again—and yet this whole journey depends upon us doing just that.

Mama can tell we're all upset and suggests we rest for a while and eat. She finds some dry grass that's hidden from view by a large bush and lays her scarf on the ground for a picnic. There are four lemons, a packet of sugar cubes, a large loaf of my grandmother's good Czech bread, and some of her homemade bacon. Honza cuts one of the lemons into quarters with his Scout knife, and my mother gives each of us a sugar cube and a section of lemon. I alternate sucking on the sugar with sucking on the lemon and begin to feel better.

After a few moments, Honza jumps to his feet.

"I'm going to walk ahead a bit to see if I can find out where we are and if we're following the right path," he announces.

We watch in silence as Honza walks up the road, bathed in the golden afternoon light. Ruzena breathes a small sigh, and I know she is also thinking about how glad she is that he's with us.

Honza hasn't gone far when the sound of a car engine causes all of us to freeze.

Seconds later, a jeep drives up the road.

Chapter 21
THE JEEP WITH A STAR

AS THE JEEP gets closer, I see something on its hood that sends terror racing through me. It is a star, a symbol that means one thing to me: Russians. This is it. We've been caught. All of our walking in the forest and Mama's codes and everything has been for nothing.

But Honza doesn't seem worried. He turns back to us and calls out, "I'm going to flag them down."

"Yes, go ahead," Mama answers.

I'm shocked. Is Mama just giving up? What about Papa? But then I realize that whoever is driving the jeep has most certainly seen us and that running and hiding would only make us look suspicious.

Honza waves his arms as the jeep draws near, and it slows to a stop just a few feet in front of him.

Ruzena and I move closer to Mama, and she puts her arms around us. "It's all right," she whispers.

We watch as two soldiers climb out—and my heart leaps when I see their uniforms.

They're American!

Two real live American GIs!

I can't believe I was so scared of getting caught that I didn't notice that the star on the jeep is white, meaning American, not red, meaning Russian. No wonder Mama wasn't worried about Honza flagging them down.

Mama introduces us to the soldiers, and I learn that their names are Private Babbit and Private Mayfield. I smile at the soldiers and stand quietly, listening to them talk to Mama. My English isn't great, but I'm able to understand some of the words they're saying. It's odd because I know Mama speaks English very well, but they seem to be having difficulty understanding each other. Finally, one soldier asks Mama a question. She answers, Private Mayfield says something in response, and they all laugh.

"What's so funny?" I ask my sister.

"I don't know. Private Babbit just asked Mama where she learned English, and she told him at school from nuns educated in England. Then Private Mayfield told her they were from somewhere called Alabama, and they all laughed."

I'm not sure why that's so funny, but it's nice to hear Mama laugh. They talk a little longer, and I notice Private Babbit is short, with a cheerful round face, and Private Mayfield is thin and tall—taller than Honza—with a kind expression in his green eyes. I can see that they are both young, probably not much older than Honza.

The soldiers start talking to Ruzena, Honza, and me, and Mama tells them that our English isn't very good, so they begin to speak more slowly and use lots of gestures so it's easier for us to understand. The soldiers tell us how surprised they were to see us, that we're in Germany but still a long way from the border post, and we weren't even walking in the right direction to get there. I wonder if the guide sent us the wrong way but figure it doesn't really matter now, because these men will help us.

"Well, ma'am," Private Babbit says to my mother, "we're going to give y'all a lift to the German post and get this figured out."

"Let's grab your things and we'll get going," says Private Mayfield, following us to the bushes by the side of the road where our suitcases are lying.

"Looks like you were having a little picnic. Would you like to finish eating before we go?" he says, indicating the scarf with the food laid out on it that we had abandoned when the jeep pulled up.

"Well, the girls were hungry, but we don't want to delay you," Mama replies.

"Please don't worry about that, ma'am. Let the girls eat," says Private Babbit.

"We're in no rush, ma'am, and it might be hard to eat in the jeep. You probably won't get a chance to eat for a while when we get to the border post, because they'll have lots of questions for you," adds Private Mayfield.

"Thank you. In that case, won't you please join us?" says Mama, gesturing to the food.

Private Mayfield looks as though he is about to decline, but Private Babbit says, "We'd be glad to. Thank you, ma'am."

We all sit around the scarf in a circle, and Mama hands out the bread and bacon. The soldiers only accept small portions, but there is plenty for everyone. Private Mayfield chews for a moment and then says, "We raise pigs and make mighty fine bacon on my farm back home, but this is the best bacon I've ever tasted."

Mama smiles at him. "Thank you. It comes from our farm in Czechoslovakia."

"You come from a farm too?" he responds in surprise.

"Yes," I say in halting English. "It's beautiful." I

don't know very many English words, but I am determined to talk to these kind men.

"Hey, you speak good English!" says Private Mayfield with a smile.

"Thank you," I say, returning his smile.

"What's your farm like?" asks Private Babbit—and just like that I am telling him about the animals in Roven and he is laughing about my "pet" geese. I use lots of hand gestures to explain what I am trying to say, and Mama helps me when I don't understand or don't know how to say something, but I am having a real conversation with two American soldiers. Pavel will never believe it!

Honza joins in, and it turns out his English is better than mine. They are curious about his uniform and tell him that there are Boy Scouts in America too.

Ruzena asks the soldiers how long they have been in Germany. They tell us they were too young to fight in the war, but they joined the army as soon as they turned eighteen and have been stationed in Germany for over a year.

Private Mayfield swallows a mouthful of food and says, "I'm proud to be serving my country, but I sure do miss home."

When the food's gone, Mama stands up, shakes

out the scarf, and puts it back in her bag. Honza and Private Babbit carry our bags to the jeep.

The jeep has no roof and no doors. There is a high bench for the back seat and two seats in front. Private Babbit climbs into the back of the jeep and offers me his hand to help me in. Then Honza helps Ruzena climb in next to me and jumps on board after her. Private Mayfield helps Mama into the front passenger seat and then gets into the driver's seat. Before he starts the car, Private Mayfield takes a small paper packet out of his pocket. He removes something thin wrapped in silver foil and hands the packet back to Private Babbit.

Private Babbit offers it to me. "Want some gum?"

I look quizzically at him. Not only do I not understand what he is saying, but I don't recognize the thing he is holding out to me.

"Don't you know what gum is?" he asks, surprised.

He removes the foil paper to reveal something flat and white that gives off a sweet smell.

"It's like candy. You can chew it, but don't swallow it." He puts the gum in his mouth, makes an exaggerated chewing motion, and nods his head. Then he points at his throat, swallows, and vigorously shakes his head. Ruzena and Honza are both watching with amused interest. Private Babbit removes three more pieces of gum from the packet and hands a piece to each of us.

I unwrap mine cautiously. As I begin to chew, a sweet minty flavor fills my mouth. It's almost juicy. I smile at Private Babbit and he smiles back. Private Mayfield starts the jeep and off we go.

The wind whips through my hair as the jeep speeds along. The road is bumpy and we bounce around, but I am tucked so snugly between Ruzena and Private Babbit that I'm not afraid.

It seems strange that I left Roven only two days ago. So much has happened that I could have never imagined—yet we still have so far to go. I long for the family I have left behind and for Papa, whom we are going to find.

It is hard to feel so many emotions tumbling over me all at once, so I close my eyes and breathe deeply. I concentrate on the sweetness of the gum. I feel the fresh air on my face and can't believe how wonderful it is to be riding in a real American army jeep—with people we can trust.

Chapter 22
THE GERMAN POST

THE GERMAN POST is a small group of single-story, whitewashed, concrete buildings. The American soldiers lead us into the main building, which is slightly larger than the others. A German officer greets us and speaks briefly with Private Babbit. Then he leads us into a small room with a table and several chairs and asks us to sit.

"May I offer you and your children some tea?"

"Yes, thank you," my mother says. "We'd all love some tea."

The officer nods to a young soldier standing at the door, and he hurries to get it.

The German officer is very kind to us and not at all like the Nazi soldiers from during the war. He tells us that we can spend the night in a nearby hotel and then tomorrow they'll take us to the refugee camp in Regensburg.

Then the officer turns to my mother. "I would like to speak with you in my office, madam. I would like to know more about your journey. It is very lucky that you decided to take that road and that the American soldiers found you."

The officer takes Mama and the American soldiers into his office, leaving Honza, Ruzena, and I alone with our tea. I sit in silence for a while, but then I can't hold back.

"I wonder why the guide told us to go the wrong way. Do you think he made a mistake? Or do you think we made the mistake by taking the road instead?"

"He may have sent us the wrong way on purpose," Ruzena says. "He seemed nervous when he left us."

"I hope our guide was an honest man," Honza says, "and wasn't trying to send us into a trap. But either way, I'm sure glad the Americans found us."

I like that Honza wants to keep the peace and make the best out of our situation. I like to think the best of people, too, but these days it is not so easy.

Finally, Mama's done talking to the officers. It's getting dark out, and I can hardly keep my eyes open. Private

Mayfield goes to get the jeep so he can drive us to the hotel in a nearby town called Zwiesel.

My body feels like it is made of lead, and it takes all my strength to walk to the jeep. Honza can see how exhausted I am, so he reaches over to carry my bag, and for the first time, I let him.

When we arrive, Private Mayfield parks the jeep, but instead of getting out, he turns and addresses Mama. "I hope it's not too impolite to ask this, ma'am, but do you have any money? The hotel is connected to our post, so it's free of charge tonight, but you will need some money when you get to Regensburg."

Mama nods. "I have plenty of German marks," she says. Then she does something very unexpected. She takes off her suit jacket and removes the shoulder pads. From each shoulder pad, she produces a thick stack of bills and shows them to Private Mayfield.

Private Mayfield shakes his head. "I'm sorry, ma'am, but that won't do you any good. The German mark was devalued this morning. That money isn't worth anything now. Do you have any other currency?"

"I have a few American dollars," Mama replies, "but I gave all my Czech crowns to our guide. I don't think Czech money would have helped us anyway."

"Don't worry. I can help you," says Private Mayfield, taking out his wallet. He pulls out a few soft green bills and hands them to Mama. "I'd like you to have this to help take care of your girls."

"That's very kind of you, but I cannot possibly accept it," Mama replies, holding the money out to him.

"Please take it. I want you to have it."

Mama nods and closes her hand over the money. "Thank you, Private Mayfield. We are so grateful for your help. I promise I will pay you back. Please tell me where I can send the money."

Private Mayfield looks at my mother for a long time. I think he is wondering if he should refuse to let her pay him back. She stares at him in the dark. Finally, he reaches into his pocket and takes out a small notebook and pencil. He scribbles something on one of the pages, tears it out, and hands it to Mama. She takes it and nods in thanks.

Private Mayfield ushers us out of the jeep and helps Honza carry our bags into the lobby. He shakes Mama's hand and bids her farewell, and then he turns to me, Ruzena, and Honza, places his hand to his forehead in a sharp salute, and says, "It was a real pleasure to have met y'all. I wish you a safe journey."

He reaches into his pocket and pulls out a new pack of gum and hands it to me. I thank him, and before he leaves, he tells me, "Thanks for telling me about your farm. It reminded me of home."

Chapter 23
WHICH WAY IS HOME?

THE HOTEL IS quiet and dark when we enter it except for one low lamp burning in the lobby. A kind woman in a dressing gown leads us up a flight of stairs and shows us to two rooms next to each other. Mama thanks her, and Honza puts our bags down in the bigger room and bids us good night.

I don't have the energy to change into my nightgown, but Mama helps me, gently pulling off my uniform and slipping my soft white nightgown over my head. There is only one large bed in our room, but I don't mind. I want to be close to Mama—and Ruzena seems to feel the same way. The three of us snuggle close together under the comforter and fall fast asleep.

When I wake up, a warm ray of sunshine is streaming in through a pair of glass doors that are open onto a small balcony filled with beautiful flower boxes. Mama is standing over the sink in the room, washing our underclothes. She wrings the water out and hangs them to dry beside the open window.

I roll over under the covers. I no longer feel sleepy, but my body still feels very tired. After a few minutes, I am drawn out of bed by the warm breeze blowing in through the door, and I long to feel the sun on my face. Ruzena is already on the balcony, leaning against the railing and looking out over the beautiful forest of pine trees surrounding the hotel. I stand next to her for a moment, enjoying the stillness and warmth.

"Which way is home?" I ask.

With a sharp intake of breath, Ruzena pushes away from the railing and points just north of the rising sun. "That way," she says softly, "and we're never going back there again."

I don't know if it would have been better if she had spoken sternly or even yelled at me, but the softness in her tone as she says the words breaks something inside of me. Tears come harder and faster than they ever have before. I run back into the hotel room and collapse on the bed next to Mama. She pulls me onto her lap and lets me cry, rocking me gently and kissing my hair.

Ruzena comes and sits next to us on the bed. I know none of this is her fault, but I can't bring myself to look at her even when she takes my hand. She hasn't held my hand since I was very little.

Eventually, my sobs subside, and Mama puts her own hand over Ruzena's hand that is still holding mine and says, "I know this has been a difficult journey, but you girls have both been so brave. I'm very proud of you, and I know Papa will be too. Today I am going to send him a telegram telling him that we'll be at the refugee camp in Regensburg. He will come get us in a few days, and then we will all be together again and everything will be all right. You just have to be brave for a little while longer, for Papa."

I look at Mama and realize how hard this is for her too. She's been brave for us for so long, and now I must also be brave for her. But I still have so many questions.

"But what about Babicka and Pavel and Maruska? Will they be okay? Will we ever see them again?"

"I hope so, my darling."

"Will they escape and come to us, or will we go home someday?"

"I don't know the answer to that now, but I have to believe they'll be all right and we'll see them again."

I must believe that, too, or I won't be able to go on. I wipe my eyes with the handkerchief that Ruzena hands me.

Chapter 24
SENDING A TELEGRAM

HONZA MEETS US in the hotel lobby on our way out.

"May I join you on your walk into town?" he asks.

"Of course!" I say, skipping along beside him. It's hard to believe that I have only known him since yesterday—already Honza seems like a big brother to me, and I feel safer when he's with us. Ruzena is trying not to show it, but I know she's pleased he's coming with us.

Zwiesel looks like a picture from one of my storybooks. Small white houses with brown and red roofs line the streets, and a red stone church with a tall steeple stands in the center of town. Green mountains rise up just beyond the buildings. As we walk to the center of town, we see that a celebration is underway. "Look at all the flowers and ribbons on the buildings!" I exclaim. "I know the pink ones are roses, but what are the yellow ones called?"

"They're called arnica. You can press them and use the juices to relieve sores and bruises," Honza replies.

"You really are a proper Boy Scout," Ruzena teases, and Honza looks pleased.

"Mmmm, it all smells delicious." I inhale deeply as we pass a stall selling freshly baked sweet buns, braided loaves of bread, and sizzling sausages.

"They must be celebrating a feast day in honor of the Virgin Mary," says Mama, pointing to a large banner featuring a picture of Mary holding baby Jesus. When we reach the town square, a brass band is playing and a large crowd has gathered around, clapping, singing, and enjoying themselves.

"There's the post office," I say, pointing to the other side of the square. Ruzena isn't paying attention. She's watching the band and swaying to the music.

"Would you like to go closer and listen to the band with me?" Honza asks her.

"Oh yes!" she replies.

"You may go, but stay together and don't leave the square. We'll come find you after we send the telegram," says Mama.

I am about to say that I want to go with them, too, but then I see the look in my sister's eye and keep silent. I watch Honza and Ruzena walk in the direction of the music. They look so happy together— and I feel a strange mixture of joy and sadness I don't quite understand. Then I turn and hurry along with Mama.

When we reach the post office, it is empty except for two clerks behind the counter. They are talking and laughing together and give us a friendly greeting when we approach them.

"What can I help you with today, madam?" one of the clerks asks.

Mama's German is very good and she answers him easily, explaining that she needs to send a telegram to Innsbruck.

"What do you think?" he says, turning to his colleague.

"Sure! I mean, you never know with telegrams these days, but it should be fine! We're happy to send it," the other man replies, handing her a form to fill out and a pen.

"Are you planning to go enjoy the celebration?" the first clerk asks me while Mama writes.

Even though I took German in school and I can understand most everything that's being said, my spoken German is not very good. But I smile at him and say, "Yes. It looks fun."

"We're going to join the party just as soon as we close up here," he tells me, nodding over at the other clerk. "You made it just in time. We're closing in a few minutes."

When Mama is finished, she pays the clerk with some American money. As we leave, he tells her, "Thank you, madam. I'll send the telegram now. I hope you and your daughter enjoy the feast."

Mama thanks him, and we head back out into the bright sunshine. It feels like our luck is changing for the better now—from Privates Mayfield and Babbit to the men at the post office, we've met such nice and helpful people. Mama takes my hand and swings it gently as we walk. We both feel lighter and happier now that Papa will know where we are.

When we reach the town square, a new band is playing and many couples are swooping around to a jaunty waltz. I scan the crowd for Ruzena and Honza and spot them almost immediately. They move perfectly in time with the music, spinning lightly past other couples in their path. When the song ends, Mama and I wave to them, and they walk toward us hand in hand with pink cheeks and sparkling eyes.

"Did you send the telegram?" Ruzena asks Mama.

"Yes. All done," Mama replies.

Ruzena breathes a sigh of relief and Honza smiles.

"I'm so glad. Can we stay and dance a little more?" she asks.

"Yes, can we? Please!" I beg.

"All right, for a little while," Mama tells us, "but then we must go back to the hotel. The car taking us to Regensburg will be here soon."

Honza bows to me and offers me his hand. "May I have this dance, miss?"

I smile and grab his hand, delighted that he asked me, and we are off in a wild polka—spinning so rapidly that the world blurs around us. We all take turns dancing with each other, and after almost an hour, we are out of breath and laughing.

It feels wonderful to have fun.

Mama looks up at the clock on the town hall. "All right, you two, it's time to go," she calls to Ruzena and Honza over the music. They leave the dance floor reluctantly and follow Mama and me back to the hotel.

When I look at them over my shoulder, I see that they are still holding hands.

Chapter 25
ARRIVING IN REGENSBURG

AS WE DRIVE into Regensburg, we cross a wide bridge, and Mama tells me the river is called the Danube.

"Like the waltz! The Blue Danube!" I hum a little of the tune.

"Exactly," Mama says.

Regensburg is much bigger than Zwiesel and looks a little like Prague. The buildings are cream, yellow, and orange, and there is a church with a double spire just like in the Old Town Square in Prague. Seeing it makes me feel extra homesick. When we arrive at the refugee camp, I see that it's actually a four-story yellow school building that has been taken over by the American soldiers for the summer. The classrooms are lined with cots so people can sleep, and the cafeteria is packed with tables and chairs. Hundreds of people are crammed together, smoking, talking, and playing cards.

Honza, Ruzena, and I find a spot on a small bench to squeeze onto while we wait for Mama, who's gone to talk to the people in charge to find out what to do next.

"Honza! Honza, is it really you?" A young man in the same Boy Scout uniform as Honza appears from the crowd, beaming at us.

Honza leaps up from the bench to greet his friend.

"Jan! I can't believe it! I thought I'd never see you again! Are you all here?" The two Boy Scouts shake hands vigorously and clap each other on the back.

"Yes! Scoutmaster Spivek and his wife and Jiri and Tomas. We all made it. We were so worried when you didn't show up. We were praying you would find another way out, but I never thought it would be so soon! You have to come see everyone. They'll be so happy you're okay. We have a few cots in one of the classrooms. You can stay with us." Jan is clearly so excited to see Honza that he has not noticed Ruzena or me.

"Yes, of course," Honza replies. "I can't wait to see them, but first, let me introduce you to Ruzena and Anna. I traveled here with them and their mother. Ruzena, Anna—may I introduce my good friend Jan?"

Jan turns to us and smiles. "I'm pleased to meet you both and am very grateful that my friend could travel with you."

Jan is slightly shorter than Honza, with warm brown eyes and dark hair. Ruzena and I both smile and tell Jan that we're happy to meet him too. Jan wants Honza to come with him right away, but Honza hesitates, looking down at me and Ruzena. Obviously Honza is not going to come with us when we find Papa, but we are connected now and it seems strange that he would leave us. I open my mouth to tell him not to go, but Ruzena stands up and speaks first.

"Go see your friends," she says, laying her hand on his arm with a confident smile. "I'm sure they're anxious to see that you're okay. We'll find you when Mama comes back and let you know what we're going to do next."

Honza smiles back at her. "Okay, but promise you'll come find me?"

"I promise," Ruzena replies. Her hand lingers on his arm for a moment longer, and when she pulls away, Honza and Jan disappear into the crowd.

Chapter 26
THE REFUGEE CAMP

AFTER A FEW minutes, Mama returns and tells us that we must speak with the commander in charge. We collect our bags and follow Mama out of the noisy cafeteria and up three flights of stairs.

Mama knocks on the door at the top of the stairs, and an American officer with short gray hair and round glasses opens it and ushers us in. It's a cramped room that looks like it might be a teacher's office during the school year, with two large desks pushed together in front of a window. A younger officer is sitting at a typewriter, tapping quickly on the keys.

The older officer invites us to sit down, and Mama introduces us. She explains how we just sent a telegram to Papa, who is in Innsbruck, and need a place to sleep for a night or two until Papa gets word and comes to get us.

The officer listens and shakes his head when Mama is through.

"I'm sorry to tell you this, ma'am, but I doubt your husband will get that telegram. You see, since the war, all the territory recovered from the Nazis has been split into four parts: one occupied by the Americans, one by the English, one by the Soviets, and one by the French. Communication between the areas is almost nonexistent. If your husband is in Innsbruck, he's in a region of Austria that is controlled by the French. And as you know, the Americans are in charge in Zwiesel."

My mother looks stunned, but she will not give up. "But the German man at the post office said it was fine to send a telegram to Innsbruck. He said he would put it right through."

"Well, I'm sure he wanted to help, and he probably tried, but I haven't heard of a single telegram going through between the French and American territories. I would doubt that your husband received the message."

"But my husband worked for the government. He was a Czech diplomat in Paris. Surely you must have some way of reaching out to your American colleagues who have diplomatic connections with the French? If they could just let someone in the French command know that we are here, I'm sure it would get to my husband."

"I wish it were that easy, but communicating with the French is almost impossible at the moment."

My mother takes a deep breath and nods. "All right, well, can you provide us with a place to sleep here until I figure out what we should do next?"

The officer shifts uncomfortably in his seat. "I'm afraid every bed is full, ma'am. We could find a place for you and your daughters to put your bags, and maybe in a day or two, a few cots will open up. Otherwise there is a small houseboat nearby that is serving as a hotel. If you can afford it, I would recommend you stay there."

Mama nods. "Thank you. We'll go to the hotel." She rises and puts her hand on my shoulder to indicate that we are leaving. But I do not stand up. I feel ready to cry. Papa doesn't know where we are, and he's not coming for us.

I look over at Ruzena, but she is staring straight ahead out the window with no expression in her eyes. I reach into my pocket and roll my pebble between my thumb and forefinger.

I gaze up at the officer, unsure what to say or do next but deeply wishing that he could help us. The officer returns my gaze for a minute, and then he stands up and clears his throat.

"Well, maybe there is something I can do. You say your husband was a diplomat in Paris? Do you by any chance know anyone in Switzerland to whom you could send a telegram? If you do, they could perhaps contact your husband in Austria and let him know you are here. The Swiss are neutral, so they never lost communication with any of the territories."

Mama relaxes her hand on my shoulder. "Thank you, sir. I do have some friends who live in Switzerland, and I would be very grateful to send them a telegram."

I let out a small sigh. Mama always knows what to do. While she writes the telegram, I look out the window and watch the Danube flow on its way. Mama seems confident that this will work, so I am hopeful too.

I've felt so many different things the past few days, it's like my emotions have been on a roller coaster! I make myself take a deep breath and try to focus on the present. I've never been on a houseboat before, and I'm excited to see what it's like.

Chapter 27
SO MANY REFUGEES

"WE HAVE TO find Honza," Ruzena announces as soon as the office door closes behind us.

"I'm afraid I don't have enough money for him to stay at the hotel with us," Mama replies as we head back downstairs.

"That's okay. He can stay here with his friends and we'll be with him tomorrow. But we have to tell him we're going now. We can't leave without saying goodbye."

"You're right," Mama says. "Let's find him and then go to the hotel."

When we emerge from the stairwell into the crowded cafeteria, Ruzena tries to hurry ahead, but Mama pulls her back.

"Wait, how are you going to find him? Did his friend tell you where their cots are?" Mama asks.

"No, but they're probably in the cafeteria now. We can go table by table and look," answers Ruzena.

As my mother and sister discuss where to start searching, I scan the room. So many tables! And all are filled with men, women, and children—people who've left their homes in Czechoslovakia in search of a freer or safer one, just like us. Then suddenly I see him sitting at a table at the far end of the cafeteria. I grab Ruzena's arm and point.

"Look! There he is! There's Honza."

Ruzena's gaze follows my finger. She grins at me, and without a word, she's off running across the room. I move to follow her, but Mama puts her hand on my shoulder.

"Let her talk to him alone. You'll see him tomorrow."

I'm annoyed that Mama's holding me back. I'm sure Honza would want to say goodbye to me too. Then I look across the room and I see them. They have moved a little way from the table where he was sitting with his friends. Honza is leaning down so that their heads are close together, and although they are not touching, they are completely connected. Mama is right. I am glad that I didn't follow Ruzena. Even from across the room, I have the strange feeling that I am intruding.

Finally, Ruzena returns to us. "Honza is glad we'll spend the day here tomorrow. His friend Jan is going to share his cot with him tonight. He says they can take turns sleeping. I hope he'll be all right." Ruzena gazes back across the room at Honza, who has returned to his table of friends.

I don't want to leave Honza behind, but I'm happy he found his friends. He acted so brave, but it must have been scary to travel without them. I can't imagine taking this journey without Mama and Ruzena, and it makes me thankful for them.

Chapter 28
BUTTER

ON THE WAY to the hotel, I notice that Regensburg looks much more run-down than Zwiesel. Mama says that although it wasn't too badly bombed during the war, there is very little money available to fix the buildings. However, the streets are clean and I notice that lots of people have planted window boxes of flowers to help brighten their houses.

As we pass a small grocery store, Mama stops and says we should buy something to eat. The store is dark and most of the shelves are almost bare. An old woman behind the counter nods at us as we enter and watches us as though we might steal something. Mama takes a loaf of dark brown bread and three apples to the counter and asks the woman for a container of milk and a little bit of lard from the refrigerated case behind her. Even though she has a hard scowl on her face, I smile at the woman as she places the food in a bag. I am so hungry that I can hardly wait to get to the hotel to eat. Suddenly she stops calculating the bill and smiles back at me.

"Do you like butter?" she asks in a voice that is much softer than she looks.

"Oh yes!" I say. "I love butter."

"Then you shall have some," she replies. She turns back to the refrigerated case and produces a large chunk of butter wrapped in paper.

"Oh, no. I'm sure it's much too expensive," Mama protests. I know she's right, but I can't help wishing we could have it anyway. In Roven, we had to make butter in secret at night during the war because Babicka was supposed to give all the cream to the German soldiers, and even now it is a rare and special treat.

I'm trying not to show my disappointment—and then I can hardly believe my eyes. The shopkeeper carefully unwraps the butter and slices off a nice-sized pat. She tears a piece of paper, wraps up the pat of butter, and puts it in our bag.

"It's my little gift to you. You look like you could use it," she says with a warm smile.

It's like she is presenting me with a treasure. I can almost taste the salty creaminess already. I am practically dancing with delight as I thank her. Mama looks like she might try to refuse, but then she looks down at me and changes her mind.

"Thank you very much," she says. "You can't know what this kindness means to us." Mama pays her with some of the American money and tucks the bag under her arm. I wave to the shopkeeper as we go back out onto the street, and she waves back.

I am learning that people can surprise you with kindness when you least expect it.

Chapter 29
THE HOUSEBOAT HOTEL

A COOL WIND blows off the river as we approach the hotel, which is a long, flat wooden boat anchored to the dock by large concrete blocks. It isn't as romantic as I pictured it to be, but it's still going to be exciting to sleep on a real boat on a river!

We are fortunate to get the last room, and when we step into it, I can feel the slight motion of the water. Our room is small but has a round window, and when I stand in just the right position, all I can see is water.

"This is wonderful!" I say, gazing out at the river.

Ruzena looks at me as if I've gone crazy. "This is what you call wonderful? Everything is damp in here, and all this rocking makes me feel like vomiting."

"Well, it is certainly unique—but I do wish there was a proper place for us to wash ourselves," Mama says, looking at the bucket of cold water we were given to clean our hands and faces.

"This is miserable!" my sister says. "Can't we go back to the camp?"

"There's no room for us there," Mama replies. "At least here we have a bed and can get a proper night's sleep."

I'm sorry my mother and sister are displeased, but I'm glad we're staying here. It would be so much more fun if Maruska were here—this would be the best place to have a real high-seas adventure. I'd be so happy to be playing with her now—and to have one of those warm down comforters from our farm.

As soon as we are settled, Mama pulls out the food and lays it on a small table beside the bed. I can hardly wait to taste the butter. Mama cuts three thick slices of bread and spreads a little butter on each one so that we can have more tomorrow. I try to eat slowly and savor every bite. I can taste the sweet cream and bright salt, and I love the rich smoothness on my tongue. Even though I feel like I'm only taking tiny bites, my portion is gone in what feels like an instant, and I can't help asking for more.

Mama gives me another piece of bread—but this time she spreads lard on it instead. I'm disappointed but know I'll be grateful tomorrow. When we finish our bread, Mama gives us each an apple. It is tart, almost sour, but crisp, and I am so glad to have a piece of fruit that I eat every bit of it except for the seeds and stem. I no longer have the empty ache in my stomach, but I'm still very hungry.

After our supper, we share some of the milk, and then Mama says it's time to go to sleep. It's so drafty on the boat that it's hard to believe it's summer. Mama makes us wear our stockings and undershirts under our nightgowns and put our sweaters on top. She pulls a thin blanket over us and sings a lullaby as we cuddle together for more warmth. I snuggle against Mama's back and soon I am fast asleep.

We all wake up early, stiff from the cold and dampness. Mama rubs my hands and feet briskly to warm them and then rubs Ruzena's too. All of my clothes feel slightly damp, and I cannot get warm. Ruzena says that her throat hurts.

Mama looks at us with concern. "Let's eat the last of the bread and butter, and then we can go to the refugee camp. We can spend the day there and then just come back here to sleep."

Ruzena brightens at the prospect of seeing Honza and does not mention her sore throat again, but I can't stop shivering. I chew my breakfast as slowly as I can, savoring the butter and hoping that the food will warm me.

Chapter 30
MAKING FRIENDS

AS WE ENTER the cafeteria at the refugee camp, Ruzena runs off to find Honza. Mama and I look around for a place to sit. After a moment, Mama takes my hand and leads me across the room.

"Come. I see Mr. and Mrs. D. You remember Mr. D, don't you? He used to work with Papa at the Department of Agriculture," Mama says over her shoulder.

I look beyond her to the table that we are heading toward and see a couple who must be a few years older than Mama and Papa. I immediately recognize Mr. D as one of the men in uniform who came to Dedecek's memorial service. Mr. and Mrs. D notice Mama at once and rise to greet her. I give a polite curtsy. They are very glad to see Mama, and invite us to sit at their table. Soon the grown-ups are deep in conversation, and I'm left to sit quietly and stare around the cafeteria.

I wonder who all these people are and where they came from. I wonder why they left their homes and where they are going.

Then I catch a glimpse of someone who looks like our horrible neighbor, Mr. Z, and I almost cry out to Mama. Did he follow us here? Is he waiting until Papa arrives so he can turn us all in together? His back is to me, and when he turns around, I feel a rush of relief—the man is a complete stranger. But now I can't shake the idea that any of these people could be spies for the Russian government. I try to put away my fears by looking for Ruzena and Honza.

I see Ruzena sitting with Honza and his friends at the same table they occupied yesterday. I wish I could go over and sit with them, but I worry Ruzena would be mad at me for intruding. Then I see Honza lean closer to Ruzena and say something. They both turn and scan the room. Honza spots me right away. He jumps up from his seat, grinning broadly. He makes his way straight toward me, crossing the cafeteria with long, confident strides. When he is almost at our table, I cannot restrain myself any longer. I hop up and run toward him.

"Honza!" I cry.

"Anna, I've missed you!" Honza laughs. "Let's ask

your mother if you can come sit with us. We're playing cards and I need you to play with me. Everyone's
cheating," he says with a wink.

Honza approaches our table and gives Mama a
polite bow. She introduces him to Mr. and Mrs. D, and
he bows to them too. I admire how Honza can go so
quickly from joking with me to being proper and polite
with Mama and her friends.

Honza turns to Mama and asks, "Would it be all
right with you if Anna came and played cards with us?"

"Of course. How nice of you to ask her." Mama
smiles at Honza. To me, she says, "Go have fun, but
come back at lunchtime."

I feel grown-up as I turn and run across the cafeteria with Honza close behind.

"Hey, guys, this is Ruzena's sister, Anna," Honza
announces when we reach the table. "Anna, these are
my friends—Jiri, Tomas, and you remember Jan from
yesterday." Honza's friends all call out greetings, and I
smile and wave at them.

"Come on, make some room so Anna can sit down,"
says Honza playfully, shoving Jan's shoulder. Jan pretends to fall out of his seat in a comically exaggerated
way that reminds me of Pavel. I sit next to Jan. Honza
sits across from me next to Ruzena.

"Okay, we're playing Steal the Old Man's Bundle. Look out for this one," Tomas jokes, gesturing to Jan. "He cheats!"

Tomas shuffles a deck of cards while Jiri hums a familiar tune. As Tomas deals, I start singing the words to the song Jiri is humming. It's a folk song that Papa used to play. Ruzena knows it, too, and soon the three of us are singing in harmony. The other boys applaud when the song is done.

"You have beautiful voices," Honza says to me and Ruzena.

"Thank you! Jiri sings pretty well too," I reply.

Honza smiles at me and then turns to Ruzena. "You told me you were a concert pianist, but you could also be a professional singer."

"Our whole family likes to sing. Anna and I learned to harmonize practically before we could talk, but the piano is what I really love. I miss playing so much," Ruzena says.

"I know you'll get to play again soon," says Honza.

"Okay, let's start!" Jan picks up his cards.

Jiri teases me about taking all his cards. Jan steals some of Honza's and hides them up his sleeve. By the end of the game, we have all dissolved into laughter. I can almost forget where we are and pretend that I really did visit Pavel at camp and that these are his friends instead of Honza's.

Jan shuffles the deck and smiles mischievously. "Okay, let's play a betting game," he suggests, dealing the cards.

We all agree, although no one really has anything to bet with. The boys each have a few Czech coins that we divide among us, but that does not seem like enough. Then suddenly I remember I have something. I reach into the pocket of my jacket and feel the pack of gum that Private Mayfield gave me. I hold it in my palm, unsure if I want to share it or not. I haven't even opened it yet. It seems so precious. I had thought I might save it and open it with Papa. But then I look around the table and think about how nice and welcoming the boys are—and how kind and generous the shopkeeper was—and decide I want to share the gum.

The boys have never seen gum either. Honza and I explain what it is, and they are eager to try it. I save a piece for Papa and a piece for Pavel, then slide three sticks out of the pack and put the rest back in my pocket. I carefully tear each stick of gum into four pieces and give two to each person sitting around the table. Now we all have something of value to bet with.

We play several hands of the betting game. All of

the boys are especially excited about winning the gum. We each win a few hands, but Honza is the best card player out of all of us and luck is on his side, so after a while he has collected a pile of coins and most of the gum. We all tease him about cheating.

"Look. See. Nothing there!" Honza laughs in protest, rolling up his sleeves. Then he points to the pile of gum and coins in front of Ruzena. "Besides, I'm losing everything I have to her." Ruzena looks pleased. She is a careful card player and only bets when she is confident she can win.

At last, only Ruzena and Honza are left with anything to bet. They stare at each other over their cards, pretending to be very serious. Ruzena consults her cards and pushes all the coins and the two pieces of gum left in front of her into the middle of the table. Honza responds by jokingly flexing his muscles and pushing his pile into the center as well. Then he hesitates, takes off his neck kerchief, and throws it on top of the pile with a grin. Ruzena raises her eyebrows at him, and then she removes a tiny silver pin in the shape of a bird from her jacket collar and lays it carefully on top of the scarf.

There is a moment of silence before they lay their cards on the table. Jan, Jiri, and Tomas burst out laughing as Ruzena ties Honza's kerchief around her neck with a triumphant smile. Honza pretends to be devastated by the loss.

Ruzena returns the coins and the gum to everyone, but she keeps the scarf. Honza looks up in mock sorrow and then grins. "It looks better on you anyway."

Chapter 31
NOODLE PUDDING

WE ARE HAVING so much fun that the morning flies by. When I see the workers bringing out food, I am surprised it's already time for lunch.

"Ruzena, we have to go to our table. Mama told me to come back for lunch," I say. I can tell that she doesn't want to leave, but after a moment, she stands up to go with me.

"Will you play more after you eat?" asks Jan.

"Sure!" I say.

"Great," Honza says. "Maybe I'll win my scarf back."

"We shall see," my sister replies.

As we cross the cafeteria, Ruzena carefully straightens the kerchief. I can see how pleased she is to be wearing it.

When we get back to the table, Mama introduces Ruzena to Mr. and Mrs. D, and then she notices the kerchief. She laughs when Ruzena explains how she won it. "I'm glad you girls have found a way to enjoy yourselves. I was afraid it would be boring for you to spend the whole day here, but we must stay around in case there is some word from or about Papa. I'm sure he'll be here by tomorrow or the next day."

Papa here, maybe tomorrow! The idea is almost too wonderful to be true.

I close my eyes and picture his tall, commanding presence in his dark-brown suit with his black hair neatly combed back and shoes well-polished. I imagine him walking into the cafeteria. Everyone would stop and notice him. I would see him right away, before Mama or Ruzena, and would run as fast as I could straight into his arms. He would pick me up and hug me close and smell like soap and tobacco and Papa.

But then I stop. What if there really are spies here?

What if someone recognizes him and sends word to the Communists, telling them where he is? Could they come and take him away? Maybe we're putting him in danger by making him come get us. But Mama wouldn't let him put himself in danger. Mama knows what she is doing and Papa is very smart. I have to believe it will be all right. I force myself to push my panicky thoughts away.

"I'm hungry," I say to Mama. "Can I get something to eat?"

"Of course," she says. "Let's go."

We walk to the front of the cafeteria with Ruzena and Mr. and Mrs. D and get in the long lunch line. When we reach the head of the line, we are each given a tray with a bowl of something that looks like a thin noodle pudding, a piece of dark brown bread, and a glass of milk. Back at the table, the grown-ups start eating right away, but Ruzena and I pause to inspect our meals. I, because I am curious, and Ruzena, because she's a picky eater.

The bowl contains noodles and raisins floating in some kind of milk. Mama says the noodles are called macaroni and the milk is evaporated milk that has a little water added to it. I taste it and think it is delicious. The raisins are sweet and chewy, and the macaroni is soft and slightly salty. I think it is a nice combination and I set to work eating happily. Ruzena does not agree. She takes one tiny taste and immediately pushes the bowl away.

"Ugh! I can't eat that. I'll be sick," she says dramatically.

I look up from my bowl at Mama, expecting her to tell Ruzena to stop complaining and start eating. Instead, Mama pats Ruzena's hand sympathetically and suggests that she eat a little of the bread and then try another bite of noodles. Ruzena nibbles miserably at the bread and takes a few sips of milk, but she refuses to touch the noodles.

When I have eaten every drop from my bowl, I ask Mama if I may eat Ruzena's portion. Mama nods and Ruzena pushes her bowl toward me. I am halfway through Ruzena's bowl when two young men approach our table. They both look very weak and thin, and one of them is carrying a small bucket. The one with the bucket speaks with a wavering voice. "Do you have any leftover food to spare?" he asks.

Mrs. D leans over and whispers, "They come around after every meal. I heard that they have been here for months. It is hard to survive that long on only the rations that are provided, but I don't think they have any money or anywhere else to go."

She straightens and drops her bread into the bucket. Mama and Mr. D do the same. I pause. I'm still hungry enough to finish Ruzena's portion. I look at the men. They have been here for a long time, and I might be leaving tomorrow. I tip the remaining contents of the bowl into their bucket. Both men nod gratefully at me and move on to the next table.

I try to imagine what it must be like to have nowhere to go, and I almost cry with relief at the knowledge that Papa is coming for us.

Chapter 32
THE BOYS' STORIES
❧

AFTER LUNCH, RUZENA and I return to Honza's table, and we laugh, sing, and play cards as if we've known each other for years. At the end of another round of cards, Jan gathers them up and begins to shuffle again. I look around the table, curious about my new friends.

"I have so many questions," I blurt out suddenly. "I know why Honza was escaping and how he got separated from you, but how do you all know each other? Where are you from? And how did you end up here?" I ask, looking at each of the boys.

"Anna!" Ruzena is shocked by my bold questions, but none of the boys seem to mind.

Honza turns to her. "It's okay. You're our friends. We can trust you."

The word *trust* runs through me like electricity. The need to trust and be trusted is as profound as the fear of betrayal. Yet somehow we are sure of each other. And will keep each other's secrets.

Jan deals the cards. I know that he is thinking that if we play cards while they tell their story, we won't look suspicious and no one will pay attention to us.

Honza picks up his cards and begins, "We grew up together in Prague."

"We've been friends since we joined the Scouts when we were eight years old," continues Jiri. "The leader of our troop, Scoutmaster Spivek, is my father. He taught us the importance of honesty, bravery, and loyalty to our country. We stuck together during the war even when the Nazis wouldn't allow the Scouts to officially operate. Our families always helped one another even in the most difficult, dangerous times."

"Tomas and I are brothers, and Scoutmaster Spivek took us in to live with his family when the Nazis took our parents away," Jan says.

"After the war, we hoped everything would somehow return to normal, but you know what happened when the Communist Party took over," continues Honza. "Our families refused to join them, and my friends and I joined the anti-Communist protests."

"When we got in trouble for protesting, my father realized we needed to leave. He got word that if we could plan our own escape, we could all stay with some friends in England until we found our own place," Jiri explains. "We got special permission to go on a Boy Scout trip to a town right on the Czech-German border. Our plan was to camp in the woods and cross the border at night. We invited Honza to come with us."

"It was terrible having to go without you!" Jan says. "We were scared we'd never see you again."

"I was scared, too, but then my grandfather told me he knew a family that was planning an escape just a few days later and I could join them at Hotel Blue Star. He said once I got to Regensburg, my uncle would send for me and I could live with him in Australia. And that family who was escaping turned out to be you," Honza finishes, smiling at me and Ruzena.

"We were so lucky to find you." Tomas turns to Honza. "After we walked across the border, we went to a German post and they sent us to this camp. We knew that lots of refugees traveling from Prague ended up here, so we hoped you'd come if you got out."

"Now we just have to wait for word from Jiri's family friends in London and Honza's uncle in Australia to find out when we can leave," Jan adds.

"How does your grandfather know our family?" Ruzena asks Honza.

"I'm not sure. He only told me that I could trust you," Honza replies.

"What about you?" Jiri asks me and Ruzena. "Honza told us you were traveling with your mother. Where's your father?"

Ruzena tells them about Papa being a Czech diplomat, about his connections to the Underground government, about how he had to escape, and that we're hoping to be reunited with him soon. I notice that she's left out a few details, but I'm surprised at how open she's being with these boys. She must really trust Honza.

When she's done talking, we sit in silence for a moment, taking in all that we have learned about one another. This morning, we were strangers, but now we've formed a bond that none of us will forget.

Chapter 33
MUSIC IS MAGIC
∽

RUZENA STANDS UP. "I need to stretch my legs a bit. I'm just going to take a little walk in the halls," she announces.

Honza jumps to his feet. "Do you mind if I join you?"

Ruzena smiles. "Not at all."

I watch Ruzena and Honza leave the room side by side, and I wonder if she should've asked Mama first. Jan interrupts my thoughts. "Did you go to the Slet this year?" he asks, indicating my uniform.

"Yes, were you there too?"

"Yes, it was so much fun," he says. I agree enthusiastically, and soon the boys and I are sharing our favorite memories from the gymnastics festival.

A few minutes later, Honza and Ruzena return, walking very close to each other and smiling broadly. Ruzena comes back to our table, but Honza stops to talk to one of the officers.

"We found a piano in one of the rooms down the hall. It's actually in tune, and Honza is asking if he can roll it in here so that I can play for everyone," she says with a look of delight on her face.

"Do you think they'll allow it?" I ask. My question is answered almost before it leaves my mouth, as Honza and the officer return to the cafeteria pushing an upright piano. Ruzena practically flies to it. Honza sets up a chair for her, and she sits down and begins to play.

Instantly, all the chattering in the room stops and everyone turns toward the beautiful music. She starts with Mozart's Turkish March. It's fast and complicated. Ruzena's fingers rush up and down the keys in a blur, and her face is taut with concentration. I look across the room and see Mama standing and watching proudly.

When Ruzena finishes, there is a moment of silence and then a roar of applause. Ruzena smiles and nods her head in acknowledgment and begins to play again. This time she chooses a Chopin prelude in E minor. It is slow and romantic.

I can feel the crowd relax. It's like they've forgotten where they are and have been transported somewhere else by the music. It is magical!

By the time Ruzena finishes her second piece, Mama is standing by my side with her arm around me. Again, there is a moment of silence followed by thunderous applause. Ruzena looks over at Mama and me and smiles as she stands and bows to the crowd. For a brief moment, she could be on a stage in Prague.

The crowd wants more. People start yelling, "Encore! Play another!" and so Ruzena sits down again. A murmur goes through the crowd as everyone recognizes the opening notes of Dvořák's famous song "Goin' Home," from his *New World Symphony*. The music wraps me in images of Babicka, Maruska, Pavel, Roven, and most of all Papa. Many people in the room get to their feet with tears in their eyes. Ruzena pauses only for a second, looking out at the crowd, and then she begins to play "Kde Domov Můj?"—the Czech national anthem. I begin to sing along, and after a moment, Mama and the boys join in. Slowly more voices pipe up all around us, and soon the whole room is singing as one. "Where is my home? Where is my home? The Czech land, my home."

By the end of the song, everyone is on their feet, and the cheering is so uproarious that it shakes the building. Ruzena's playing has brought everyone together and given even the saddest and most discouraged people hope. I am in awe as I watch dozens of people rush up to thank and congratulate her.

"Your sister is amazing!" Honza says, wiping away tears.

After a while, Mama makes her way through the people surrounding Ruzena and politely removes her from the crowd. When they return to our table, all the boys stand and applaud. Ruzena smiles and gives a little curtsy.

"That was wonderful," Mama says. "But I think we need a little quiet family time, so I've decided that we should go back to the boat now and have our dinner there."

For the first time, Ruzena does not protest against the idea of leaving Honza. She's clearly worn out from the emotions of playing. I also think she's hungry—and happy at the prospect of having something other than the noodles in milk to eat.

"We will see you boys tomorrow. Good night," Mama says to the boys.

"Bye, guys! You better be ready to lose at cards to me tomorrow!" I jump up to leave.

"In your dreams!" Jan jokes with me, while Ruzena lingers behind for just a moment longer, and I know she is saying a special goodbye to Honza.

Ruzena catches up to me and she is practically skipping. She links her arm through mine as if I'm her best friend. I look at her in astonishment. This is the first time she has ever done something like this. I smile at her and she returns my grin.

As we walk along the streets of Regensburg, Ruzena is unusually talkative.

"How does Honza's grandfather know our family?" she asks Mama.

At first, Mama looks as though she might be upset that Ruzena knows about this connection, but then she explains, "Honza's grandfather worked at the Department of Agriculture when your grandfather was prime minister. Papa and I did not know him well, but we knew he was a good man, so when our contacts said he was looking for a way for his grandson to leave the country, I decided it would be all right for him to come with us."

"I'm so glad you did," Ruzena says. "He says he has to go live in Australia with his uncle, but that's so far away. If he can't get in touch with his uncle, maybe he could come with us when we leave with Papa."

Mama smiles kindly at Ruzena. "Honza should be with his own family, but we'll see what happens when Papa gets here."

I think it would be nice if Honza could come with us, but Ruzena seems totally fixed on the idea. Honza feels like family to me now, but he must want to be with his real family as much as I want to be with mine.

Chapter 34
DREAMS OF HOME

WE STOP TO buy food at the same shop we went to yesterday, but there's an old man behind the counter today, and he doesn't offer us any butter. Mama buys a loaf of bread, three more apples, a chunk of hard cheese, and some milk. We carry the food back to the boat.

The air has gotten cool and raw, and it begins to pour just before we reach the houseboat. Ruzena and I are both shivering by the time we reach our room. Mama wraps the thin blanket around us, but it feels damp, like everything in the room. Mama rubs our hands to warm them, but we cannot stop shivering. This is nothing like playing Storm at Sea.

Finally, Mama sighs and stands up. "We can't stay here tonight. Mrs. D told me that there's one proper hotel left in town. We'll get a room there, and we can have warm baths and a better night's sleep. Even if it is more expensive, it'll be worth it to keep you from getting sick. Let's go."

A real bath! It sounds like heaven! It takes only a minute to collect our bags, and we follow Mama back out into the rain.

The hotel is a large stone building in the center of town. It was clearly a very fancy hotel before the war, but now one side of the building is in ruins and boarded up. It must have been bombed. The other side of the building is still standing strong, and they have done their best to make it look neat and presentable.

We enter the lobby, and Mama asks for a room and hands over the last of the money from Private Mayfield. The woman behind the check-in desk nods politely, picks up a key, and leads us down a long hall and up a flight of stairs to our room.

The room is like a dream come true. It's warm and comfortable. There are two large beds covered in fluffy down comforters and a bathroom next door with hot running water. The only problem is that it seems like the bathroom must have been a room for washing clothes before it was turned into a bathroom, because instead of a bathtub, there are two enormous sinks. At first, I am so disappointed that I almost burst into tears, but then Mama points out that the sinks are large enough that we can actually fit in them with our legs bent. Mama suggests we bathe first and then eat our dinner and go to bed. I can hardly wait for Mama to fill the sink with warm water. It feels like forever since I've felt clean.

I submerge myself as much as I can in one of the sinks. Mama finds a soft washcloth and some soap and gently scrubs my back. My muscles relax and I finally feel warm. I tilt my head back into the other sink, and Mama turns on the warm water and soaks my hair. Then she rubs my scalp with some sweet-smelling shampoo. As she rinses my hair clean, I think this is the most wonderful bath I've ever had.

After Ruzena and Mama bathe, it's time to eat. We use the desk by the window as a dining table. It is dark now and the rain drives hard against the glass, making it impossible to see outside. Mama draws the curtains. It feels safe and cozy in the room. Mama divides the bread and cheese into three portions and gives us each an apple. We take turns drinking the milk out of the bottle. Tonight there is enough for us to eat until our bellies are satisfied. It feels wonderful to be clean and warm and full. When we are done eating, a heavy drowsy feeling begins to overwhelm me, and I crawl into bed next to Ruzena. I am asleep before Mama turns off the light.

The next morning when I wake up, I feel like I've

slept for days, and it takes me a minute to remember where I am as I snuggle under the comforter.

Ruzena's still fast asleep next to me, but Mama is sitting up in her bed looking through some papers. I slip out of bed and climb in next to Mama. She puts her papers aside. "Did you have a good sleep?" she asks.

"Yes, very good," I reply.

"Did you have a good dream?" she asks. It is a question that both Mama and Babicka used to ask me every morning at home. I close my eyes, trying to bring forth the images of the happy dream.

"I was in Roven—picking strawberries with Maruska. When the basket was full, we gave some to Babicka and Pavel and Teta J. Then Maruska and I went to the gazebo and sat down to eat some berries. They smelled so good, but I woke up right before I could take a bite. Oh, Mama, I miss Maruska and Babicka and everyone in Roven so much."

Mama kisses the top of my head and says, "*Hodná holčička*. You are such a brave girl. I dreamed I was riding horses in Roven with my sisters. It is so bittersweet to dream of home." Mama sighs.

Bittersweet sounds like a taste, not a feeling. I roll the word around in my mind, wondering what it means exactly. At that moment, Ruzena sits up in bed with a

start. She looks around for a moment before she real-
izes where she is.

"I was dreaming that I was playing the piano at a
concert in Prague. I was fantastic. All the clapping and
cheering woke me up," she says, and then she laughs
self-consciously.

We all look at each other for a moment. Savoring our dreams of home, wishing we didn't have to let
them go.

Chapter 35
DASHED HOPES

WHEN WE ENTER the cafeteria, someone is playing folk songs on the piano.

"Come on, let's find the boys," Ruzena says to me. She turns and hurries off, but I stay and listen to the music with Mama for a moment. The presence of music has changed the atmosphere in the room. People sing along or tap their feet and seem much friendlier. I think the music reminds people of home—and gives them hope for the future.

I look around expecting to see Ruzena already sitting with Honza and his friends at what I now think of as their table. To my surprise, Honza and the other boys are not there, and Ruzena is speaking urgently to a man who is sitting at the table with a woman and two small children. The man is shaking his head at my sister as though he is sorry that he can't help her. Ruzena then turns away from him, and I see her eyes searching every table for Honza.

Mama spots Mr. and Mrs. D, and she leads me across the room toward them, but we are intercepted by one of the American refugee workers. He politely informs Mama that the commanding officer has asked to see her in his office as soon as possible. Mama says she will come right away, and then she tells me to run and get Ruzena. I move as quickly as possible through the crowded room. When I reach Ruzena, I am slightly out of breath.

"Come quickly! The commanding officer wants to see us right away," I tell her, pulling at her arm.

"I can't find Honza," she says in a daze.

"You can look for him later," I tell her. "Maybe Papa is already here!"

This brings Ruzena back into focus. "Papa!" She takes my hand and we hurry back to Mama.

We're all so excited at the thought of seeing Papa that we practically fly up the stairs to the office. Mama knocks, and when the commanding officer opens the door, we walk in trying to be calm, but we're shaking with anticipation. However, the room is empty except for the officer. He invites us to sit, and we stare at him expectantly.

"Madam, I'm sorry to inform you that your telegram was reported as undelivered, which means your contact in Switzerland did not receive it. Communication is still so difficult these days."

Mama continues to talk with the officer, but I don't hear what they're saying. There is a rushing sound in my ears. The room seems to spin. Papa is not here. He is not coming. He *still* doesn't know where we are. There's no way for us to contact him.

Then I think of our predicament. We have nowhere to go. We are stuck here just like those men with the bucket begging for extra food.

I feel like I can't breathe. I reach for the pebble in my pocket, but it's gone. I know it must have just fallen out at the hotel or something, but it feels like a sign—a bad sign.

Somehow, the meeting with the officer ends, and Ruzena and I follow Mama back downstairs and into the cafeteria. People call out to Ruzena, asking her if she'll play again. She doesn't even look at them. How could it have only been yesterday that she created such a spirit of hope in this room with her music?

"What happened? Is your husband on his way?" asks Mr. D when we reach their table.

Mama shakes her head and repeats what the officer said. Then she says, "We have no money left and nowhere to go, but that's not the part that worries me the most. I'm afraid if he doesn't hear from us, he'll think we didn't make it out and he'll try to go back to Czechoslovakia to find us. If he goes back, I'm sure he'll be caught and then . . ." She trails off, looking at me and Ruzena.

"No, no, I'm sure he knows better than to go back. You mustn't worry. We'll help you figure something out, and in the meantime, you may stay with us," Mrs. D says kindly. "We've been given a teacher's office to sleep in, and I'm sure we can make room for you."

I remember that Mama told me that Mr. D is a very important figure and the American officer gave him and his wife a room to stay in while they awaited information about their next move. It is very generous of them to offer to share their space.

We follow Mrs. D up a flight of stairs and down two hallways. When we reach the room, she opens the door. "It's not very big, but I hope you can make yourselves comfortable," she says, holding the door wide for us to enter. The room has two cots squeezed side by side, two wooden chairs, and barely enough floor space for all four of us to stand together. I know we are lucky that they are generous enough to share their space with us, but I cannot imagine how all of us are going to stay in this tiny room.

"You can put your bags under there," Mrs. D says, indicating the space under one of the cots. "I will go ask if there are any more blankets and pillows, and then we can make you girls a cozy little place to sleep on the floor." She smiles warmly at us and pats my back. I force myself to smile back and thank her as she leaves the room. She is a very kind woman, but it does not take away the awful, empty feeling I have inside.

I want to ask Mama what we're going to do, but I don't want to hear that she doesn't know, so I sit quietly on the edge of one of the cots. Ruzena sits next to me. She hasn't said a word since we left the office. Mama removes a small sewing kit from her bag, sits on one of the chairs, takes off one of her stockings, and begins to repair a tear in the leg. I watch her for a minute and then turn to stare blankly out the small window.

I let my mind wander to the last time I saw Papa.

"Anna, come give me a hug," Papa calls. Gar and I run across the lawn, and I jump into his open arms. He scoops me up and holds me tight. "Oh my goodness! You're getting so big, I can hardly lift you anymore!"

Gar runs in circles around us, and Papa bends over without putting me down and scratches Gar behind the ears. "I have to go now," Papa tells me. "Are you going to be a good girl for Mama and Babicka?"

"Yes, of course!" I say.

"Good. You're such a big help to them, Anna."

"But when will you be back, Papa?" I ask.

Papa looks at me for a moment and then says, "I'll see you soon. I promise." He puts me down and kisses the top of my head. "Hodná holčička," he whispers, and then he is gone.

I am startled when Ruzena jumps up from the bed. I quickly rub the back of my hand across my eyes so no one can see my tears. We are all afraid. We all feel lost. We all want to go home. But now is not the time for my tears.

Chapter 36
NO TIME FOR GOODBYES
∽

"MAMA, MAY I go look for Honza?" Ruzena asks, standing by the door.

Before Mama has a chance to answer, Mrs. D enters carrying two flat pillows and some gray wool blankets. "Honza?" she says. "The young man you traveled with that we met yesterday?"

"Yes," says Ruzena.

"He's not here. I'm afraid he left last night."

Ruzena stares at Mrs. D as if she does not understand what she's just said. "No, no, that's not possible. You must be mistaken. Honza would never leave without telling me."

Mrs. D smiles sympathetically. "Oh, my dear, I'm sorry, but I'm pretty sure it was him who left. I heard that he got word from his uncle and that he had to leave at once," she says.

Ruzena shakes her head. "But he wouldn't leave without saying goodbye. No."

"I'm sorry that we didn't get to say goodbye to him, but it is very lucky that he heard from his uncle so soon," Mama says gently. "We should be happy for him." Ruzena sinks back down onto the cot and continues shaking her head.

"What about his friends?" I ask.

"I'm afraid I don't know," Mrs. D replies. "I haven't seen any of the other boys today."

Ruzena sits frozen on the bed. It's like she's afraid to feel anything right now. I know how she feels. I believed that we'd made it. I believed that Papa would come and get us and that we'd find a safe place to stay until we could go home.

And we both believed that Honza would stay in our lives.

I catch Ruzena's eye and we exchange looks. "He would *not* leave without saying goodbye," she says.

"We *will* hear from him again," I tell her.

Chapter 37
BITTERSWEET MESSAGES

RUZENA GETS UP and pulls on my arm, so I stand up next to her. "Mama," she asks, "I think I might go play the piano for a little while, if that's all right? Anna will come with me."

"You may go." Mama looks up from her sewing, a bit surprised. "But don't be gone for too long."

"Okay," Ruzena agrees. "We'll be back soon." She leads me out of the room. Once the door closes behind us, she leans toward me and says, "We're going to look for Honza."

"What?"

"Mrs. D might be mistaken," Ruzena says. "Let's at least see if we can find one of his friends to ask what happened."

Ruzena starts hurrying down the hall to the stairs, and I have to run to keep up. "We have to check all the rooms. The fourth floor is where the offices are, so we won't go up there, but we'll start on the third floor and work our way down to the cafeteria."

We walk up and down the halls on the third floor, peeking into crowded rooms lined with cots. There are many boys wearing Scout uniforms who are about Honza's age—but none of them are him or his friends. Every now and then, Ruzena stops someone and asks if they have seen Honza, but all her inquiries are met with regretful shakes of the head. Some people compliment her on her piano playing, and she thanks them before hurrying on.

The dull gray hallways on each floor seem endless, and the faces blur together as I try to keep up with my sister. I feel trapped in a maze. Finally, we finish searching the ground floor, and Ruzena sinks onto the bench we sat on when we first arrived. I sit next to her, still looking into every face hoping the next person to enter will be Honza.

After a while, my sister stands up. "He's not here. Let's go back to the room."

We walk slowly, neither of us totally ready to give up. When we reach the bottom of the stairs, we hear a familiar voice. "Anna, Ruzena, wait! I've been looking all over for you."

"Jiri! You're here! Where's Honza?" Ruzena cries.

He's about to answer when Jan appears at the end of the hall and calls out, "Jiri, come on! Your father says we have to leave right now! Bye, Anna and Ruzena!"

"I'm sorry," Jiri says. "I have to go." He presses a folded paper into each of our hands. "These are from Honza. His uncle sent for him yesterday and he had to go immediately, but he made me promise I would give these to you."

Then Jiri shakes my hand. "It was very nice to meet you, Anna. I hope you keep singing."

"You too and good luck," I say. Jiri turns and runs down the hall toward his friend.

Ruzena returns to the bench, and I follow her. I watch her unfold her letter, a sad half smile on her face.

I turn away and focus on my own note. The message is written in a hurried scrawl.

Dear Anna:

I'm sorry we won't get to say goodbye in person. My uncle sent me a ticket to meet him in England and from there we'll sail to Australia. I hope it won't be anything like your "Storm at Sea" games! I'm so happy we got to *travel together. I always wanted a little sister and now I feel like I've got one. I hope we'll see each other again someday. Thank your mother for me and tell her I said goodbye! Stay brave and stay strong. Good luck finding your father and your new home.*

   Your friend, Honza

Knowing that he thought of me as a little sister makes me happy and sad at the same time. The word *bittersweet* pops into my head, and now I know what it means.

I sit quietly next to Ruzena, giving her some time alone with her letter. When she finally looks up, I ask her, "What did he say to you?"

"He says he will come to London in a few years to find me. I told him my dream is to study at the Royal College of Music in London after I finish high school."

For once, I don't have to ask any questions. I know we both desperately want that to come true. We stand and walk back to our room together, feeling closer to each other than ever before. This journey really has changed us.

When we enter the room, Mama and Mrs. D are just where we left them. Mama looks up and sees Ruzena's pale face.

"Ruzena, are you all right?"

Ruzena nods as she sits back on the bed. "Honza is gone, but he said goodbye."

I hand my note from Honza to Mama so she can read it, and sit down next to Ruzena. She relaxes her body against mine, trusting me to hold her up.

Chapter 38
MOVING ON

THERE IS NOTHING to do now that the boys are gone, so we stay in Mrs. D's small room. I take each item out of my bag and put them back in again, hoping that touching my belongings will help me feel less lost, but it doesn't work. Ruzena reads Honza's letter over and over again, folding it up and smoothing it back out each time. Mama mends another pair of stockings while Mrs. D reads next to her. It has started to rain again, and I watch the drops hit the window and slowly roll down like tears.

A short knock breaks the silence. Ruzena jumps up and opens the door. A perfectly groomed officer stands at the door. He has a thin black mustache and his black hair is slicked back under his cap. I can tell by his uniform that he's not American, but I'm not sure where he is from.

Mama gets up and speaks to him softly, and I'm

pretty sure they're speaking French. My French is terrible, so I have no idea what they are talking about. The officer gives my mother a polite smile and a bow. She closes the door and turns to Ruzena and me.

"Gather your bags, girls. We must go quickly," Mama says while putting on her hat.

"Who was that? What did he say?" I ask.

"He said, 'Madam, I'm sure you understand why I can't introduce myself, but how long will it take you to get ready?' I told him we could be ready in two minutes. He said we could have longer if we needed because he never knew a lady who could be ready in two minutes, but we must hurry."

"How do you know we can trust him?" Ruzena asks the question that is always in my head lately.

"I just believe we must," Mama answers. And there is nothing more to say.

We gather our bags, bid farewell to Mrs. D, thank her for her kindness, and follow Mama out into the hall.

Mama says, "The lieutenant said we must walk out of the building, turn left, and get into the back of the first car. He is giving us papers so that we can travel with him as his family. I will be his wife and you will be his daughters. I think he will help us find Papa. Come along quickly now."

My heart is pounding in my chest, but I try to hold my head high as I walk behind Mama and Ruzena.

We pass the rooms packed with people waiting to move on, wanting to go home.

Chapter 39
THE CHAUFFEUR
∽

THE RAIN HAS stopped and the sun is trying to push through the clouds when we leave the building. The street is busy. Cars rush past, and people come and go. I watch them and wonder what they see when they look at us. Will they believe we're a French family?

The car is waiting just as the lieutenant said. The French officer steps forward with a little bow, opens the back door of the car, and holds it wide for us to get in. Mama slides in first, then me, then Ruzena.

I'm worried and tired as the lieutenant closes the door firmly behind us and gets into the front passenger seat, next to a chauffeur wearing a black cap.

We're in another car with another stranger we have to trust.

Then the officer looks over his shoulder and says, "I believe you know my driver." The chauffeur turns to face us.

"Papa!"

Chapter 40
ANOTHER BORDER

MY HEART LEAPS with joy—I can actually feel it! We all reach out for Papa, and he reaches back and squeezes our hands. I want to jump into Papa's arms, to hug the lieutenant, but I have to wait because we still have to drive to the border.

"How did you find us, Papa? How did you know where we were?"

"I got your telegram. The one you sent from Zwiesel," Papa says.

"From Zwiesel?" Ruzena is shocked. "But the American officer said that was impossible. He said no communication was going through."

"But the man at the post office in Zwiesel did say he could send the telegram," I remind her.

Papa nods and continues, "I got the telegram, but I still wasn't exactly sure how best to proceed, and then I ran into the good lieutenant here, who was in Innsbruck for some meetings. We were friends when I was a diplomat in Paris, but I hadn't seen him in years. I explained our situation to him, and he kindly offered to help me obtain some French passports and come with me to get you. Now we must hope those papers work to get us across the border."

We tell Papa all about our journey as we drive. After about two hours, Papa stops the car at the border. An officer leans in and asks to see our papers. He looks at them for a moment and then asks the lieutenant to go with him into the border office.

I sit completely still and quiet. I was so happy to see Papa, I forgot we still had to make it across another border. Mama's hands are clenched tightly in her lap. Papa's hands are wrapped around the steering wheel, and he sits staring straight ahead. Ruzena clutches Honza's letter. It seems like my family doesn't draw a single breath while we sit in the car on the German-Austrian border waiting for the lieutenant to return from the patrol building.

The minutes drag by like hours. I shove my hands into the pockets of my jacket as far as they will go, and my finger pokes into a tiny hole in the bottom corner. Something hard rubs against my fingertip. I move my hand around, trying not to tear my pocket any further as I dislodge my pebble. I can't believe it was in there this whole time! An officer passes by the car and pauses to look us over. He can tell we're not French, I think. He knows we are lying and he is going to report us. I stare directly into his eyes, clutch my pebble, and pray that he doesn't speak to us. Then the French lieutenant reappears. He nods to the officer and gets back in the car.

"Drive on," he says. Just two simple words, but to me they are the most beautiful words in the world. They mean we're on our way to the French headquarters in Innsbruck.

We are together.

We are safe.

Chapter 41
FINDING HOME
∽

THE WATER FEELS deliciously cool as I float gently on my back gazing up at the velvety green Austrian Alps. The ones in the distance are capped with snow, and they remind me of fancy cakes sprinkled with powdered sugar. I roll over and swim slowly to the wooden raft floating in the sparkling lake. I pull myself out of the water and lie flat on the smooth planks. I wave to Mama and Ruzena, who are lying side by side on the beach, reading.

I think of Honza—and how lucky it was that we met him. He showed us that in the midst of uncertainty, you *can* find people you can rely on. He seems impossibly far away now, but I trust we will see him again someday.

The sun has baked the surface of the raft, and I close my eyes to shut out the brightness. I want to just enjoy the moment and melt into the warmth—but one thought still circles around inside my head and I can't let it go. Where will home be now?

The French officers have been kind and generous to us, and staying at their headquarters has been like a wonderful dream, but it can't last. We are leaving in a few days. Papa says we've been invited to stay with some of his friends in France, near the Swiss border, where he will look for a job.

I am glad he has a plan for us, but it is all so hard to imagine. And when I asked if we'll see Maruska or Pavel or Babicka again—if we will ever go home—Mama said she prays we will, but for now, as long as the four of us are together, wherever we go is home.

I push myself up on my elbows and squint to see Papa walking down to the water in his bathing suit. He stops next to Mama and Ruzena. Mama reaches out to him, and he takes her hand and kisses it. Then he bends to kiss Ruzena on the top of her head. She looks up at him and smiles.

Papa smooths his black hair off his forehead and waves at me. He takes a running start and dives into the lake with a big splash. With swift, easy strokes, he swims out to the raft.

"Come on in, Anna," he calls to me.

I stand up. Papa holds out his arms and I jump. The water is perfect. Together we swim out into the lake.

GERMANY

Pilsen

Hotel
Blue Star

Chudenice

Klatovy

NO-MAN'S-LAND

REGENSBURG

Zwiesel

ANNA'S JOURNEY

Teta J's Hotel

Roven

○----------●----------●

PRAGUE

CZECHOSLOVAKIA

LEGEND

———————— BY CAR

– – – – – – BY TRAIN

- - - - - - ON FOOT

AUSTRIA

AUTHOR'S NOTE

The real Anna & Ruzena

This book is based on the true story of my mother's escape from Czechoslovakia at the age of eleven in 1948. Her real name is Jana, although we call her Anna in the book. It is a story that I have heard all my life and it is a part of the fabric of who I am. When I was little, it simply sounded like an exciting adventure, and I played it like Anna and Maruska play Storm at Sea. As I grew older, I began to think about the terrifying reality of my mother having to flee her homeland because it was no longer safe, leaving behind almost everything and everyone she ever knew and loved. I thought about the strength and bravery it took for my grandmother to take her daughters on this journey not knowing if or when they would ever find my grandfather. I thought about how versions of this story have played out again and again all over the world, not only throughout history but also today. And I realized how important it is for my children to understand that.

A few years ago, I recorded my mother telling the story to my children. She began by saying, "This is the story of how you all came to be." After listening to the recording, I decided to write this book for my children and my nieces and nephews so they would know where they came from. I embellished some of the plot and combined several of many cousins to create Anna's cousins, Maruska and Pavel, but most of it happened as I have written it.

The historical parts are as accurate as possible. My grandfather (Papa) really did act as a spy for the Czech Resistance during World War II. He communicated with British Intelligence via the BBC radio to tell them where the Nazi munitions factories were so they could bomb them. It is also true that the Communists wanted him to join their party, and when he refused and then uncovered the truth about the death of Jan Masaryk, they put out a warrant for his arrest. He had to leave the country right away. His friends from the Underground Resistance set up an escape for him, but they refused to take children. He and my grandmother didn't want to be apart, but they wouldn't leave the children behind, so after he left, another escape was planned for my grandmother, mother, and aunt using codes such as the book *Wuthering Heights* and "buying kid gloves." With these codes, the men orchestrating the escape would be able to recognize my grandmother and she would know whom to trust.

It turned out that they should not have trusted their guide through the forest. My mother found out almost forty years later that many refugees sent on escape routes from Hotel Blue Star were purposely sent into traps and caught by the Russian police and sent to prison camps. My mother believes that they avoided the trap because of the mud and their decision to take the drier road.

After they reunited with my grandfather in Regensburg, they stayed at the French command in Austria for a few weeks. From there they were taken in by the generous family of a Swiss poet and diplomat, Francois

Fanzoni, whose daughter they had hosted when she came to Prague to study voice. After nine months in France, my grandfather was offered a job in French-occupied Morocco. They lived in Morocco for six years. From there, my grandfather got a job working for the United Nations High Commissioner for Refugees, and he and my grandmother lived all over Europe, finally settling in a small town in France near the Swiss border. My mother went to college at La Sorbonne in Paris and then got a scholarship to study biology at Harvard-Radcliffe University. She met my father at Harvard and decided to stay in the United States.

My grandmother begged her mother and sisters to escape, too, but they didn't want to believe the Communist takeover was going to last. Eventually, my grandmother convinced her sister (Teta J) to leave. She and her daughter (Maruska) tried to escape a few months later, but they were caught. Teta J was put in a prison camp for women. Maruska was put in an orphanage until she was found and rescued by one of her aunts, with whom she lived while her mother was in prison. The farm in Roven was taken away from my mother's family by the Communists.

Because of the Iron Curtain, my mother was not able to return to Roven until 1990, more than forty years after she left. The farm was in terrible disrepair, but some of her family, including her cousin (Maruska), still lived nearby. They were overjoyed to be reunited.

Over the years, the family has regained some of the farm property in Roven, although not the main house, and they are slowly rebuilding. In 2016, I traveled to Roven with my parents, my husband, and our two children. My mother and her cousin showed us their old school and where they played the Mrs. games and Storm at Sea. They took us to the same churchyard where their grandparents were buried. My mother and my daughter led the whole family in singing "Koupím Já Si Koně Vraný" and "Zeleni Hajove." My children played in the fields with their cousins just like Anna, Pavel, and Maruska. It felt like home.

ACKNOWLEDGMENTS

First, thank you to my mother, Jana Moravkova Kiely. Thank you for knedlíky, buchty, and Honza stories, and for playing Storm at Sea with me, for singing all the songs, and for talking about Roven so I knew it before I ever saw it, and thank you for all the millions of other reasons I grew up and wanted to write this book. Thank you for, while I was writing the book, always remembering more stories and more details even when you said you couldn't. Thank you for staying up past your bedtime to read my drafts. Thank you for saying it was because you wanted to see how it turned out—even though it's your story. Thank you, Mommy.

Thank you to my father, Robert Kiely, for believing in me from the very start, for instilling in me a deep love of books and writing, and for teaching me how to tell a good story.

Thank you to my wonderful editor, Nancy Paulsen,

for guiding me through the journey of writing my first novel with infinite wisdom, kindness, and understanding. I am deeply grateful for the extraordinary care you took in making my mother's story blossom. I learned so much more from you than I could have ever imagined.

Thank you to my wicked-awesome sister, Christina Kiely, for so many things that I'd need to add an addendum to fit them all in, but mostly for always being there when I need you.

Thank you to my first reader and editor, Mary Sullivan Walsh, for all your work helping this book take shape, for your energy, and for your friendship. You made me believe my dream could be a reality.

Thank you to my beloved writing professor, Adrienne Kennedy. You taught me the joy of living in my imagination, the importance of never giving up, and, of course, how to write.

Thank you to the amazing team at Penguin Young Readers. I am in awe of all that you do. Thank you to Sara LaFleur for your patience and kindness in answering all my questions and helping me every step of the way; thank you to Emily Romero for taking a chance and working your magic; thank you to Allyson Floridia for your incredible attention to detail; and thank you to Luisa Rivera for creating the most beautiful cover art I've ever seen, which perfectly captures the essence of the book.

Thank you to all my fabulous family and friends for all your love, patience, and enthusiasm. Especially: Majka and Milo Kiely-Miller, for asking the best questions; Katie Kanter, for being one of my first readers and giving such insightful comments and suggestions; Sarah Pershouse, for always listening even when that meant taking a three-hour walk so I could tell you the entire plot of the book before I started writing; and Sarah Olsen, for being the world's best cheerleader all the time.

Thank you to my super-fantastic kids, Nina and Sam. You inspire me every day. Happiness is snuggling up under a blanket, reading aloud to you. I love you a million, billion, zillion bunches!

Finally, thank you to my incredible husband, Chris Ilch. I don't even know how to find the words to say thank you for everything you do and what you mean to me, but fortunately you can read my mind, so I don't have to! LYIEEWWAB!